Dirt Tracks

To all the kidz at
Italia Conti —

Dirt Tracks

Enjoy- Martina Murphy

Martina Murphy

POOLBEG

Published 2000 by
Poolbeg Press Ltd,
123 Baldoyle Industrial Estate,
Dublin 13, Ireland
E-mail: poolbeg@iol.ie
www.poolbeg.com

A catalogue record for this book is available from the British Library.

ISBN 1 85371 908 0

The Arts Council
An Chomhairle Ealaíon

Illustration: Leonard O'Grady
Cover design by Artmark
Set by Pat Hope
Printed and bound in Cox & Wyman Ltd.
Reading, Berkshire, UK.

Biography

Born in 1968, Martina Murphy's passion for writing started early. She began writing her first novel *Livewire* when she was just fifteen. It was published in 1997 by Poolbeg. She has since penned *Fast Car* and *Free Fall*. *Dirt Tracks* is her fourth novel for teenagers.

Martina is married with two children and lives in County Kildare.

Acknowledgements

Thanks to all the usual suspects. For a full listing buy the rest of me books!!

*This book is dedicated to the memory of
Nana D'arcy*

Prologue

My Hero

My Hero is my big brother. He is 13. He tells me loads of stuff' bout cars and driving. He wants to be a rally driver when he gets big and so do I. He makes me laugh and he mopped up all my blood when some big boys hit me and he hit the big boys back for me. He is tuff and smart and has millions of friends.

He is what I want to be like when I am 13.

Billy Donnelly. Aged 6.

Part One

Chapter One

The screeching woke me. That, and the cheering.

Rubbing me eyes, I looked at the alarm clock. 1.30am. I guessed that would make it about two in the morning. The alarm clock was always wrong. I liked that, it fitted in better than a normal clock would have.

The cheering was getting louder and the screeching noise was coming closer. I jumped from bed and climbed across Nick's bed to get a good view out the window. Headlights from a car were careering crazily across the road, left to right and back again. They lit up the crowd gathered on both sides of the road. Everyone was cheering and going mental, slapping the car on the roof and on the bonnet. The car did a handbrake turn in the middle of the road, spun fast until its headlights were facing away from me and then I saw it properly.

Wow!

Jesus H. Christ!

Where the hell had Nick – 'cause it had to be Nick – got hold of a *Porsche?*

I groped about in the dark for me jeans and shirt. I was down the stairs and out the front door in seconds.

Nick, me brother, grinned at me from the window of the car. "Knew you'd be down," he laughed. "Isn't she a beaut?" He was sitting like some kind of king behind the wheel. One hand casually holding the steering wheel, the other dangling out the window.

The car was purring like a huge satisfied cat. The sound of money.

Awe. That's the best word I know to describe how I feel when I see cars like that. That's how I felt. I touched her, smooth and cold. The perfect body of the ultimate driving experience. "She's a beaut." I looked at Nick. "Where d' you get her?"

"Just off Dame Street." Nick opened the door. "Hop in and I'll give you a spin."

Some of the other lads tried to push their way in but Nick told them to "Feck off". He didn't have to say it again. They watched in silence as I climbed inside.

The seats were white leather. The dash was bare. This was a driving car. "Rev up." I grinned at Nick. "Let's see what she can do."

Zero to 100 in seconds.

I dunno how long I was driven around for. It wasn't long enough. Nick's a great driver and we took off at speed, up the long straight stretch of road that separates our estate from the private houses in the next one. The speedometer climbed and the car glided.

Reaching the end, just about to slam-bang into a wall,

Nick brought the car around in a graceful, high-pitched handbrake turn and we took off, back in the other direction. Over and over again he did it. I wanted to drive forever.

Then he let me drive her. Just once. But that's all I needed. High and fast and mental.

Eventually, the petrol gauge began to blink and the car began stuttering. Cursing, Nick stopped it and we were swamped by the others again.

"Here." Someone shoved a petrol can at Nick.

"Cheers." Nick doused the car in petrol.

Jesus!

It always ended like this, but did it have to? She was a gorgeous piece of machinery, loved and cared for. Polished and cleaned. And she could fly . . .

"Eh, Nick . . ." I said.

"Yeah, yeah," Nick's eyes were glazed now. He shoved a box of matches at me. "You can do it this time."

There was a collective gasp from the other lads gathered about. To be picked to light a car was an honour, to be picked by Nick . . .

Everyone was watching me. I opened my mouth to say something but the words wouldn't come. All I could do was stand and stare dumbly at the box.

"Go! Go! Go!" A chant started in the back of the crowd.

I turned the matches over in me hands. I looked at the car which still gleamed despite the hard driving. Lastly, I looked at Nick.

I tried to tell him with my eyes that I couldn't do it but he just kept grinning at me. Then, he began to chant too, clapping his hands and raising the crowd into a bigger frenzy.

I wanted to have the courage to throw down the box but I couldn't humiliate Nick like that, so, me hands shaking, I lit the match.

"GO! GO! GO!"

I closed me eyes . . .

"GO! GO! GO!"

And threw it at the car.

The petrol caught at once and she began to burn. The smell of oil and burning leather filled the night air.

A huge cheer went up and everyone kept coming over and slapping me on the back.

I couldn't open me eyes.

I knew I shouldn't have done it. A car like that . . .

In that instant, I knew that somehow what I'd done was bad. I didn't want to be like Nick anymore

Chapter Two

Smoke filled the room. Hid his head in wreaths of grey which curled upwards only to be replaced by more smoke when it began to abate.

Whiteser thought the boss looked like some kinda dragon, which was fitting. He was known as the Big Smoke. CB language for city. The Big Smoke wanted the city. But everything in its own time.

"Donnelly?" Smoke barked.

Whiteser gulped. Smoke unnerved him. He scared just about everyone. "He lifted a Porsche last night. Cut clean through the alarm, a nice job."

"And?" More smoke.

Whiteser took a slug of Carlsberg in an attempt not to cough. "He drove it home, did the usual fancy drivin' and burned it."

Smoke nodded slowly. "I want him."

It was an order.

"But – "

"I – want – him."

Whiteser stood up. He wiped his sweaty palms along the length of his jeans. "We'll get him."

"Good."

As Whiteser left, Smoke permitted himself a small smile. Nick Donnelly was class. Four years lifting cars and cop-dodging. Caught just once and on probation. Smoke knew Nick was going to be good for him. Smoke knew that he and Nick could make a good team. Smoke knew where Nick's weak spots lay. Smoke knew Nick like the back of his hand.

Just like he knew all his men.

Chapter Three

I couldn't sleep that night. I was even awake to hear Ma and Da come in from their night out. Both were boozed. Da was loudly setting the world to rights and Ma was giggling and laughing. I liked to hear her laugh. Eventually, they climbed into bed and I heard them click their bedroom light off.

I was awake when daylight began to filter through the curtains. I heard the rumble of the bin-truck as it drove into the estate. Nick's always saying that he'd love to drive a bin-truck. And he will too. Nick wants to drive everything, just once.

He slept like a log, grinning in his sleep, one of his arms dangling out of the bed, his feet poking out at the end. I wished I could sleep as easy but every time I closed me eyes the image of the car kept popping into me head. I know what I'd done was wrong, but I don't know why. I mean, I've seen cars burnt before and it never bothered me, but this car made me feel different.

At about seven thirty, Ma got up. She kept moaning away about the head on her. I guessed that she'd be in rotten humour that day, she always is whenever she goes out drinking with Da. Not that she goes out with him that often or anything, but he'd "taken the bookies to the cleaners" the day before and him and me Ma had gone off gargling to celebrate.

Still, at least her being sick might mean that she wouldn't make . . .

No.

She was going downstairs and me heart lurched as I heard the sound of the kettle being filled and the rattle of the frying-pan being taken from the press. Come hell or hangover, Ma was determined to make porridge.

The disgusting smell of porridge being cooked on a frying-pan filled the house. It wasn't fair. I'd been hoping she'd oversleep and forget to wake me for school.

Ten minutes later, up the stairs she came, her step careful. Normally she bangs on the door and yells at the two of us to get up, but today, because of her hangover, she just poked her head around and sort of whispered, "Billy – school."

I pretended to be asleep. She came in and pulled the curtains. The light hurt me eyes. "Up." Her voice was sterner this time.

"Aw, Ma, I feel sick."

"*Up.*" She folded her arms and attempted to glare at me. "I'm the one should be in bed," she muttered. "I'm the one who feels sick."

She did look sick. Her face was white and her eyes were red. Her black hair, which she normally wears in a scraggy pony-tail was nearly sticking to her face with grease. "I'm sick," she said again, pointing to herself.

"Yeah, but you probably had the enjoyment of gettin' plastered to feel like that." Nick was grinning at her from his bed.

She rolled her eyes. "Cheeky brat." Going over to him she gave him a shove. "And you might as well get up and check if there's any work for you down the job centre."

"Sure, sure, Ma." He could talk to her anyway he liked and she'd laugh.

She never laughed at me.

"Hey, is that a car at the top of the road?" Ma was squinting her eyes against the sun and peering out the window.

Nick sat up. He made a big deal of looking where she was pointing. "Yep," he confirmed. "Looks like it."

"I hope you had nothing to do with it. You're still on probation from last time." I could see her tensing up, her fists curled and her shoulders sort of hunched about her ears. "Nick?"

"Yeah, yeah, Ma." I dunno how he had the nerve to smile at her. Climbing out of bed he tweaked her hair. "Now, where's me porridge? Nothing like a bowl of porridge to set you up for the day – huh?"

She laughed at him but she still looked worried. "Please Nick, say you weren't involved."

13

"Aw, Ma, you worry too much." Her grinned at her as he left the room. "Go and get me somethin' to eat, there's a good woman." He laughed at her indignant expression.

I wished I could charm her like that. But no such luck. She pulled the covers off me and said sharply, " Billy, how many times have I to tell you – get up – you'll miss school if you don't."

"That's the idea," I mumbled.

"*Up!*" She waited until I was out of bed before leaving the room.

I sat on the edge of the bed and rubbed me eyes. Nick came back in and, whistling away, he began to get dressed.

The words were out before I thought about them. "You never should've done it." I couldn't look at him.

Nick paused in the middle of pulling on a sock. "What?"

"You never should've burnt the car."

He laughed. "Sure, right, whatever you say."

He was waiting for me to smile back but I couldn't.

"Anyhow," he leered, "it wasn't me that set it on fire, was it?"

"No, it wasn't." I glared at him. "It was me and I feel crap about it. Don't ask me ever to do that again."

There was a silence. Nick broke it. He sounded a bit hurt. "So it's all right for me to rob the feckin' thing, it's all right for me to drive you around in it, but it's not all right to burn it and get rid of me fingerprints?"

14

"That's not the reason you burnt it." I tried to explain. It was hard. "You only burnt it 'cause you wanted to."

"Yeah," Nick nodded, considering. "Yeah, that too, I suppose."

"Yeah, well, I didn't want to burn it. It felt all wrong or somethin'."

"Aw, get a grip, Bill." Nick made a face at me. Then, changing the subject abruptly, he said, "Come on, you'd better hurry. It's nearly half eight. You'll miss school."

He gave a bit of a laugh when he said that. Nick left school when he was fifteen after failing just about every subject in his Junior. Da said there was no point in Nick being in school and he'd be better off in a job.

Nick still hasn't found a job to suit him. He lost the last one about eight months ago. It was an all-right job too, stacking shelves in a supermarket. I dunno what happened exactly, Nick wouldn't say. I guess he just fought with his boss, like all the other times. He can't stand being ordered about. So now he's jobless and loving it.

I passed me Junior and me Ma thinks I'm a genius now. I didn't even do brilliantly, just a few D's and C's. I got a B in English though. Ma thinks I'll be the next Roddy Doyle and make piles of money, so every day she makes me go to school.

I waited until Nick left the room before looking out the window. The car was a burnt-out shell at the top of the road. I really felt sick when I looked at it.

Chapter Four

I gave it ten minutes. I figured that if I left it ten minutes, all Ma's porridge would be eaten or gone cold. She makes piles of porridge every morning, heaps of it. She reminds me of that old woman in the story I used to read when I was a kid, the one who couldn't get her magic porridge-pot to stop making porridge.

Me and Nick can't get our Ma to stop doing it either. It's like she's obsessed with cooking the stuff.

She cooks other things too. Weird things. Da thinks she's marvellous when she concocts bizarre curries and stuff but Nick and me, we stay well clear.

I dunno how we're still alive, we eat next to nothing.

It was going on for eight-fifty when I got into the kitchen, so I had the excuse of being in a rush.

"Gotta go," I said. I pulled on me jacket.

Ma was sitting at the table having a smoke. Calmly she pointed to my porridge bowl. "You can't go to school on an empty stomach," she said. "Eat up."

Nick grinned at me from across the table.

I picked up the spoon and shoved some porridge in me mouth. It tasted really sweet and I gagged.

"Honey," Ma beamed. "I put honey in it. I read somewhere that it's good for you."

I grabbed a glass, shoved it under the tap and filled it with water. "Nice," I said, trying to wash the taste out of me mouth. "I really have to go now."

Nick stood up as well. "Me too."

"But you haven't finished either," Ma wailed. "No wonder you boys are so skinny."

Ignoring her, Nick and I made for the front door.

"It's the better way to start the day!" she yelled after us.

Nick slammed the door closed and rolled his eyes. We both started laughing at the same time. "I can think of a better bleedin' way," Nick joked, taking a packet of fags from his pocket and offering me one.

I took one and Nick lit it for me. He smokes *John Player Blue*. They're all right but I prefer stronger ones. Still, Nick gets the dole, so he's the one with the cash. I can't tell him what fags to buy.

There was a real smell of heat in the air. It was one of those misty days, cool in the morning, but by lunch-time the sun would have come and burned all the mist up. Then it'd be a scorcher. Nick peeled off his jacket and tied it around his waist. Even wearing his jacket like that, Nick looked cool. He's the classic tall, dark, handsome guy. Every girl in our estate fancies him, but he ignores them. He says it's better to have no ties where we live. I dunno what he means but I pretend I do.

No one fancies me. I don't blame them. If I was a girl I wouldn't fancy me. I'm small, have dark longish hair and a face covered in freckles. Me personality wouldn't do much for anyone either.

We were coming to the top of our road. The Porsche was still smoking. The smell was petrolly and rubbery. I like that smell. As we got nearer, I did me best not to look at it. Every step made me heart thud down further into me feet.

Two lads were walking around the wreck. I recognised the taller one – Whiteser. Everyone knew Whiteser. He's called Whiteser because he's an albino. White hair, white skin and sorta pinkish eyes. The other guy with him I didn't know but he was about the same age as Nick.

"Oy!" Whiteser startled me with his shout. "Donnelly – you do this?"

Nick stopped. So I did too. I saw Nick shove his hands deep into his pockets and shrug. "What's it to you?" Nick's voice was even.

I stuck me hands in me pockets.

"Porsche, was it?" The guy I didn't know moved towards us. He had dirty blond hair and the word *hate* stamped across his knuckles.

"Coulda been."

"You did a good job lifting that."

"I didn't say I lifted it."

I wanted to go. These guys gave me the creeps.

"Can I have a word?" Whiteser came towards us now. He had a stone in his hand and was tossing it casually from one hand to the other. Staring at me, he added pointedly, "Alone."

"We were just going," I found my voice. Even though I tried to sound hard, like Nick, I didn't. I tugged Nick's sleeve.

"*You* were just going, squirt," the other guy leered at me. "Run on now."

"Hang on here a sec," Nick said. He moved nearer to me. "We *were* just heading off – right?"

The stranger gave a smile. "It's to your advantage," he said. He raised his eyebrows. "What we've to say is very much to your advantage."

"Let's go, Nick." Again, I pulled at him.

Nick didn't budge. "Yeah?"

"Yeah," Whiteser nodded.

I gulped. "Nick?"

"Lose the kid." Whiteser again.

I couldn't believe it when Nick gave me a gentle shove. "Hop it, Bill. I'll see you later."

"But – "

"You heard," the stranger said.

All three began to walk away. From the back, Nick didn't look as mad-lookin' as the other two.

There was nothing I could do. I hoisted me bag on me shoulder and began the walk to school.

I don't mind school, sometimes it's a good laugh. I don't know many people in my year though. Most of the guys I hung around with left after their Junior, or else they decided to do Transition Year. I didn't bother with that. All I want is an education so I can get a job and earn some cash. The sooner I do me Leaving the better.

I'm in fifth year.

I just about made it on time. Miss Malone hadn't even arrived. She's our tutor and a real babe. She can't control a class though – everyone keeps talking all over her and firing bits of rolled-up paper at her. We take our biros out of their tubes and use the tubes to blow the bits of paper up the class. Malone has fuzzy hair and all the paper lodges in it. It's mad, so it is. Like mega-dandruff only worse.

I got in and sat beside Tom. He's all right, lives in the private estate, but he's good craic. He was bent over his Irish 'ecker'. "You done these?" he asked, holding out the book.

"Yeah." I fumbled about in me bag and dragged out me copy. "Here."

Tom grinned and began to flick through the exercise book. "I owe you."

He was always saying that. I rolled me eyes and began messing, trying to shove his arm every time he started to write so that he'd have massive scribbles all over his page.

"Feck off, will ya," he shoved me back.

"Good weekend?"

20

The voice caught me on the hop. Clara Daly, the girl who sits on the other side of me in most classes, had arrived. She's gorgeous. Shiny brown hair, shiny brown eyes, shiny laugh. Not a bad body either. I cursed meself for acting like a fool in front of her.

She grinned at me and Tom. "Well?"

I went red, like I always do when she talks to me. My feeble personality descends into no personality at all. I shrugged and tried to think of what to say.

"All right," Tom said. "Went to a gig." He was still scribbling furiously.

"And you?" Clara turned her eyes on me. "What did you do?"

"Aw, nothin' much," I muttered.

"The same nothing much you do every weekend?"

She was laughing at me. Her eyes sparkled when she laughed. I wished like anything she wasn't laughing at me. But she was. I didn't know what to say. I half-thought of telling her that I burnt out a beaut of a car the night before, but nah, I didn't think it'd help my cause. "Pretty much," I nodded. "I never do anything much."

Clara smiled over at Tom, who was still gawking at me Irish homework. "He should come out with us some Saturday night, shouldn't he, Tom?"

I nearly puked. She had to be joking.

"What the hell is that?" Tom pointed to a word.

"Agam," I clarified.

"You should come out with us," Clara said. "It's good craic. We usually head to someone's house or maybe to a film or somewhere." She stopped and her voice went a bit funny. "Why don't you come?"

Me tongue was in knots. Me eyes were all over the place. I wanted to look at her and I knew if I did, I'd melt into the ground or something. So I shrugged. "I, eh, don't have much cash, you know." I wanted to say that because it was true and also, because I was afraid she was kidding me. I'd die if she was.

"Oh." She blinked. She shrugged. "Well, sometimes you don't need any. But anyway," she waved her hand about, "it's OK, it was just an idea." She turned away then.

I think I'd messed up but I dunno how I did.

She acted really weird the whole of the rest of the day.

Chapter Five

"So?"

Whiteser nodded. "It's all set. He's in."

Smoke smiled, took out a cigar case and offered it to Whiteser.

Whiteser knew better than to refuse. He chose a cigar and shoved it in his mouth and waited as the boss lit it.

Soon the two men were smoking in silence.

"Any problems?" Smoke asked casually. "Like how 'in' is he, really?"

"He was a bit off at first, but then little brother was mentioned."

"I see."

"He mellowed a lot when I mentioned his money for hanging around. Fifty quid a week. I gave him three weeks up front, like you said."

"Good." Smoke nodded. "Keep the workers happy, ey?"

"Yeah." Whiteser was choking on the cigar. He coughed and tried to stop himself. But he couldn't. Coughing and spluttering as his boss looked on impassively, he gasped out, "He said he'll lift the cars and drive."

Smoke laughed. Then he stopped. Stabbing his cigar out, he stood up. "He'll do whatever I tell him," he snapped. Voice harder, he repeated slowly, "He'll do whatever I tell him."

Chapter Six

I bunked off the last class today. It was only religion so it didn't matter. Our religion teacher is a header. She's separated and living with an ex-student and has a kid by him. Not that that's mad or anything but the fact that she teaches religion cracks everyone up. The class is usually totally out of control with everyone asking her her moral standpoint on just about everything from contraception to Brussels sprouts. Normally I enjoy it, but today I just couldn't get Nick out of me brain. I was afraid Whiteser was going to beat him up or something. All I wanted was some quiet where I could think without being hauled up for not paying attention.

It was about half three when I headed out of the school grounds. The day was really hot and I pulled off me jumper and stuffed it in me bag. I dumped me bag behind a tree where I'd pick it up later on the way home. Now that I was free I didn't know where to go, so I decided to head over to the big shopping centre and maybe have a gawk in the record shop or just sit down somewhere and think.

I was crossing the green towards the shops when I saw it. There's this garage at the far end of the green and outside it was parked this brilliant green BMW. It had alloy wheels that gleamed in the sun and low-profile tyres.

I was like some kind of a zombie walking over towards it. When I stood in front of it, all I could do was stare.

"Beauty, huh?"

A man in oily blue overalls had come up behind me. He stood, arms folded, grinning down at me.

"I was just lookin'," I said, feeling defensive for some reason. "I never touched her."

The man grinned. He spread his hands. "All I said was, isn't she a beauty?"

"Yeah, well . . ."

"Three-litre engine," he continued. "She'd rip the road out of it."

"She's got fuel injection too."

"Yep, a right little goer." He slapped the roof affectionately. "Have to do a service on her." He glanced at me. "Want to see inside?" He opened the door and beckoned me over. "Isn't this class or what?"

At first I didn't want to go near the car, but then, me legs seemed to want to go of their own accord. Inside, it was black seats and high technology. "Nice," I shrugged.

The guy laughed. "You been in a lot of these babies

or what?" he scoffed. "Nice, me arse." He seemed amused. "Nice," he laughed again.

I didn't like that he was laughing at me. I started kicking the ground with me foot and glowering.

"She's due a service, want to see the engine?"

"What?" Fecker, trying to make a laugh of me.

The man turned away. "Just thought you might be interested, that's all. I saw the way you were looking at her, and well . . ." His voice trailed off. He opened the car door to let himself in and stared out at me from the driver's seat. "I was like that about cars as a young lad. I know what it's like."

"Wouldn't mind." The words were out before I could catch them.

The man grinned. "Hop in, I'll just drive her into the garage."

I grinned back. Maybe today wouldn't be so crap after all.

It was after five when Paul suggested that I leave the garage.

I knew Ma would be planking herself wondering where I was, but every time I thought of leaving, I couldn't. I mean, this guy had some great cars and he was letting me look inside them and look under them. It was brilliant.

"I think you'd better be heading off now."

It wasn't said like he was pissed off with me being there or anything. He said it as if he knew I really did have to go.

I took me head out from under a Merc we'd been working on. "Yeah, I guess so." I rubbed me oily hands along me trousers and Paul laughed and tossed me a cloth.

"Your mother'll be pleased with the state of you tonight."

I smiled back and started to clean my hands. Paul was siting on an upturned box and he was studying me hard. I looked down at the ground. People staring at me made me uneasy.

"You know a lot about cars – don't you?"

I shrugged. "I read a lot. Car maintenance books, magazines." I tried to rub the oil off me trousers with the rag but they ended up looking worse.

"You actually buy car maintenance books?"

"Eh – me older brother gets them and I read them when he's finished." Nick's an expert in shoplifting books that he wants.

"Well, you certainly know your stuff. I'm impressed."

I said nothing.

"Call back anytime."

"Yeah?"

"Once it's not during school hours – OK?"

Fecker, it was none of his business anyhow.

"Deal?" Paul was looking at me again.

I wanted to tell him to shove it. But I couldn't. It had been one of the best afternoons of me life. If I played me cards right, I could come again. "Tomorrow after school?" I wanted to puke at the eagerness in me voice.

"Sure."

"Great." I tried to look as if it wasn't a big deal. "See you then." I didn't wait for him to reply, just took off down the green running like mad. Ma was going to go mental I was so late. Plus, I had to rescue me schoolbag from the ditch.

Chapter Seven

It was well after five when I did get home. I let meself in with my key and tried to sneak upstairs before anyone saw me. I actually managed to make it halfway up before I heard her storming from the kitchen into the hall, where she stood, hands on hips, glaring up at me.

"Ma." I tried to smile calmly, like Nick would.

"And where the hell were you 'til this time?" Without waiting for an answer, she shrieked, *"And your dinner is ruined!"* She came up the stairs and caught me by the elbow. "Come on before it's burned altogether."

I let her drag me into the kitchen. Da and Nick were already there, sitting in front of empty plates.

Ma took a plate of respectable-looking chips out of the oven where she'd been keeping them hot. Then with a flourish she took a burger out and put it beside the chips.

"Bought from the chipper by your brother," she announced, beaming at Nick.

"We're celebratin', aren't we?" Da smiled proudly and patted Nick on the back. Then, glancing at me, he said, "Go on Nick – tell Bill the big news."

I was confused. Nick and Da were usually at each other's throats.

"I've, eh, got a job, Bill." Nick stared down at his hands.

"Yeah?" For some reason, I felt sick.

"It's, eh, to do with cars."

"Don't be so backward," Da boomed as he gave Nick a dig in the ribs that nearly sent him flying off his chair. "That's what's wrong with the two of you." He looked at both of us. "No confidence. Sell yerselves." Looking encouragingly at Nick, he said, "Now tell Bill exactly what you told us."

"Yes, go on, Nick," Ma smiled proudly at him.

Nick wouldn't meet my eye but he said loudly, "It's a mechanical job, working with cars and telling people exactly what kind of car would best suit their needs, stuff like that."

"Oh, right."

"Well?" It was my turn to get a shove off Da now. "Isn't it great?"

I stared across the table at Nick. I opened my mouth but nothing came out. All he did was to look challengingly back at me. There was silence while I wondered what to say. In the end, I pushed me chips away. "Listen Ma, I'm not hungry. I don't feel the best."

Ma looked anxiously at me. "You all right?"

"The boy's fine." Da, wasting no time, began to divide me chips up between him and Nick.

"Yeah, I'm fine." I tried to smile as I stood up. "Honest, I'm grand. I'll just head upstairs."

"Do you want some tea or anything?"

"Naw."

"Do you want a sambo?"

"Naw."

"Crisps?"

"No, honest Ma."

"Some eggs?"

"Mayro, the lad's not hungry," Da said. "Leave him alone."

"Did you get fed somewhere else?" Ma was peering into my face.

"Naw."

I'd just made it to the kitchen door when it must've dawned on her to wonder why I'd been so late home. "Hang on a sec," she asked. "Where were you 'til this time anyhow?"

"Aw, I just bunked off the last class and went for a walk."

"Billy!" Ma said aghast.

She was about to launch her usual "Education is so important" lecture when I said, "It was only religion."

"Load of crap," Da laughed. "Waste a the boy's time." He turned around in his chair. "That's what you say if anyone asks why you bunked off, just tell them it's a loada crap."

I half-smiled. Da was always giving out about his own horrific education at the hands of some religious order or other. "I will."

"Fair play. Fair play."

Ma didn't look reassured. "Will you get into trouble for bunking off?"

I shrugged. "Suppose." I decided to go for broke. They were in good form. "Well, " I said, "There won't be any trouble if you write a note to say I came home 'cause I was sick . . . or something." I looked hopefully at them.

"I dunno . . ." Ma frowned.

"Get out a pen an' I'll write it." Da was in great humour. "The lad has initiative, Mary, so he has."

I would've preferred if Ma had written the note but beggars couldn't be choosers. I rummaged in me bag and pulled out a copy and a pen. I tore the middle pages from the copy and handed the paper and pen to Da.

"Leave them there." He indicated the table. "I'll get around to it when I've finished." He shoved the remainder of my dinner into his mouth. Picking up the teapot and beaming at Nick, he asked if he'd like some tea.

I slunk out and slowly climbed the stairs to me room. Lying on the bed, I stared at the ceiling. I grinned as I thought that at least now I wouldn't get into trouble for bunking off. Thoughts of Nick made my smile disappear. There was something not right –

"Hiya, Bill." Nick coming into the room startled me.

He walked over to his bed and picked up a magazine.
"Here, got you this today." He tossed a car magazine
onto me bed. "It's the latest one."

"Thanks."

"You could be a bit more excited about it. It's the
latest issue, there's a great piece on . . ."

"You rob it?" I interrupted.

"No, dawww." Nick made a face. Putting his finger to
his lips, he dipped his other hand into his jeans pocket
and pulled out three £20 notes. "I paid for it."

I wished he'd robbed it. "Jesus, where did you get
that cash?" I felt sickened. I wasn't sure I wanted to hear
the answer. I sat up in bed and stared at him.

Nick shoved the money back into his jeans. "Advance
payment in me new job." He gave me a wink. "It's cool,
Bill, really it is. All I have – "

"Are you workin' for Whiteser?" I asked and when
he didn't answer I said softly, "Stupid question, 'course
you are."

"Workin' with Whiteser," he snapped. "Not for him."

He stared at me and I stared back at him. He was the
first to drop his gaze.

"Are you mad? Are you?" I asked.

"No," he replied earnestly. He went over to the
window and looked out. His voice was hard as he said,
"I'm sick of havin' no cash – right? There's nothing to
the job, all I have to do is find cars and drive for them –
no big deal."

I shook me head and bit me lip. "Nick – "

34

"It's what I do already only now I'm getting paid." He turned to face me and his voice almost sang, "It'll be great having a few quid. I can give Ma money and get her off my back about getting a job." A smile hovered about his lips as he added, "And I can even start to bond with the oul fella."

That made me grin a bit. "Right."

"And I can give you some, Bill. You'll be able to go out and have a few pints with your mates."

"I don't want any of it."

He plonked himself down beside me. "Sure you don't?" He dangled a twenty in front of me face. "It's me last offer – goin' . . . going . . ."

I have to say I was tempted. Twenty quid. It was the most I'd ever been given in me life.

"Me last offer?" Nick began to fold the twenty up into smaller and smaller pieces.

"All you have to do is drive?"

"Yep." He was still folding.

"What do they need the cars for?"

"Aw, feck's sake Bill, I dunno."

"Great job."

"Yeah, it feckin' well is – right!" He jumped from the bed. "It's the best bloody job I'll ever get."

He threw the money at me. "I wanted you to have it – I thought you'd be thrilled."

Now I felt awful. Nick was great and I had enough crap in my life without fighting with him. And, I guess, he was probably right. With a failed Junior Cert behind him, plus the fact that he was on suspended sentence, employers were definitely not going to be queuing up to offer him work. And maybe it would be OK. Maybe the job would be brilliant . . .

"Sorry." I said. I picked up the £20. "Thanks." I pointed to the magazine. "And thanks for this too. Now get lost until I read it."

"Don't order me about," Nick grinned. "I'm the breadwinner in this house and don't you bleedin' forget it!"

I didn't think I would.

Aloud, I laughed and said, "About bleedin' time too. I was beginning to think you were useless."

Nick pounced on me and we began to wrestle. We fell off the bed and landed on the floor with a thump.

"I thought you were sick, Billy!" Ma's voice cut through the messing. She was standing at the door.

"Eh – I don't feel as bad now." I pulled myself up and aimed a kick at Nick who grabbed me foot and pulled me back down. I hit the floor with a bang. Nick and I laughed.

"Will you stop going on like kids!" Ma snapped. She waited until we were both on our feet before continuing, "Your Dad wants a hand with that letter for school, Billy. He wants to know what he has to say."

"Oh, right."

"And seeing as you're feeling fine, I'll stick something on the pan for you."

I heard Nick guffaw behind me. "It's all right, Ma, I don't feel hungry."

36

"You must be starving," she declared. "Sure you haven't eaten since lunch."

"Yeah but . . ."

"Just go and help your dad and I'll have something nice for you then, all right?"

"Great," I tried to inject some enthusiasm into me voice. I couldn't look at Nick, who I knew was laughing. Instead, without looking back I followed Ma downstairs.

Da was in the front room, sitting in his chair in a haze of cigarette smoke. His brow was creased up in concentration and he was chewing me pen in frustration. Racing results were displayed on the Aertel screen. His bulk seemed to fill the whole room.

"Billy," he greeted and beckoned me over. "What exactly is it I have to say in this letter?"

"Maybe Ma should write it," I tried to suggest tactfully.

Da looked offended. Pointing to himself, he said, "I said I would and I'm not going to let you down."

That'll be a first, I thought.

"Now," Da took a deep breath and raised the pen in the air looking for all the world as if he was going to attack the piece of paper. "What's this teacher I have to write to?"

"Miss Malone."

"Fine – Dear Miss Malone," he laboriously wrote down each word in his large scrawl. He looked expectantly at me, "What next?"

I frowned. I wanted to keep the letter as short as possible, otherwise I'd be there all night. "Please excuse William's absence from class today," I composed. "He was sick and came home."

Da looked puzzled. "William?"

"Yeah, that's what the teachers call me in school."

"William, me arse. You're Billy. What sort of an eejity name is William?"

"Well – "

"Anyone would think you were feckin' royalty." He stabbed at the paper. "I'm going to write and insist that they call you Billy." He glared at me as if it was my fault. "No son of mine is going around getting called William."

Even though I knew there was no point in arguing, I couldn't resist saying, "It's on me birth cert, Da."

"Yeah, only 'cause the flippin' girl in the registry wouldn't write down Billy. So we said, write down William so that we could shorten it to Billy – see?"

"Yeah."

"You're Billy and that's *that* – right?"

"Uh-huh."

"Now," he settled down again. "What was it you wanted me to write?"

"Please excuse Billy's absence from classes today. He was sick and came home."

"Right." Da bent over the page, stuck his tongue out of his mouth and began to write. He paused and stretched after the first sentence. "I hate writin'," he groaned. "It gives me headaches. Get us a cuppa, will you, Bill?"

"Sure." I exited to the kitchen, determined to get back quickly. Da's spelling was terrible and I wanted to correct it before he finished the letter. When I got to the kitchen, Ma was piling some sort of food onto a plate. "Just some eggs for you," she said brightly, getting out a knife and fork. "Eggs are good when you're sick."

"Eh – thanks." I pointed to the kettle. "I'll eat them in a sec. I've to bring a cuppa in to Da."

Ma giggled. "Have his brains exploded from the concentration yet?" She shoved me into a chair and ordered me to eat. Then she marched in to Da and told him to come out and make his own tea and not to be using me as his slave.

I could hear Da laughing and cursing at the same time. "Get me tea, woman, and justify your existence."

She cursed back. But with a grin on her face, she came out and put the kettle on.

I liked when they went on like that.

Da came out a few minutes later. I'd just managed to swallow some egg when he threw the letter down beside me. "Finished," he declared. He gave me a thump. "Now do us a favour and ask your mother to write it the next time."

I picked up the letter and glanced at it. What I saw made me cringe. Da had written what I'd told him but he'd underlined my name about a million times and written: *Call my son Billy or elce their will be trouble.*

Then he'd signed his name in huge letters.

That was all I needed! I'd have to scribble it out.

I wondered if maybe I could get Ma to write another letter without Da knowing. But she'd never go behind Da's back. She'd look all prim and say something like, if your Dad's note isn't good enough for you then tough. Maybe Nick . . . but nah, Nick's writing was almost as bad as Da's. No, I'd just have to hand this yoke in.

"Eat up." Ma broke into my suicidal thoughts.

"I wrote you a grand note, didn't I, Bill?" Da was beaming at me, looking for approval.

"Yeah, thanks." I shoved some more food into my mouth and tried not to taste it.

"What's that you have there?" Da came over with his mug of tea and examined my plate. "Eggs – lovely." Turning to Ma he said, "Hey, Mayro, rustle us up some of those, will you?"

I wondered for the millionth time what Da's stomach was made of.

"Here, have mine." I shoved my plate away and said, "I'm full Ma – thanks."

Without waiting for her to answer, I ran upstairs and grabbed the magazine Nick had bought me. Locking the bedroom door, I settled down for a night's reading.

Chapter Eight

Some great job Nick had. He was still snoring under the covers when I got up this morning. Apparently he'd told Ma that his day started at twelve.

What a chancer.

I'd woken up last night when he'd come in. He was locked. He'd gone out on the tear with his mates and they'd done a pub crawl, Nick had paid for most of the gargle and drunk most of it too by the state of him. He'd fallen down the stairs and I'd had to get up and help him climb into bed. He'd fallen asleep fully dressed and I was the one Da had yelled at for making noise.

There was no way Da was going to be yelling at Nick anymore, not while Nick had betting money in his pocket.

I had to face Ma's porridge alone at breakfast. She sat and stared at me as I ate. The silence between us grew a bit uncomfortable. Ma doesn't seem to be able to talk to me when we're on our own. I always feel as if I've done something to make her mad.

Eventually she said, "Nick was in a bad way last night, wasn't he?" She lit a fag and didn't look at me as she talked.

"Yeah," I attempted a smile. "Totally locked." I hoped she'd keep talking – that way I could get away with not having to eat too much.

Ma nodded and said softly, " It's a funny way to be carrying on, going in with a hangover the first day in his new job."

"Aw, well, you know Nick – "

"What?" Her sharp voice stopped me mid-sentence. "What's that supposed to mean?" She didn't let me reply, just went on, "What do you mean by that?" Her voice rose, "Are you trying to say there's something wrong with your brother? Are you?"

"No, I – "

"Good." She stabbed her cigarette out on a saucer. "Good."

"Ma, I – "

"Just because you're still in school, don't look down on the rest of us."

Her words stung. "I don't." I turned from her angry face and stood up. "I've gotta go now."

She said nothing as I went in search of me jacket, didn't even give out to me for not finishing me breakfast. She didn't even say good-bye to me as I went out the door.

Walking to school in our estate is awful. I don't mind when I've Nick beside me but when I haven't, I get scared.

42

I tried to look cool as I began the walk up the road. I slung me bag over me shoulder, shoved one of me hands into me jeans and began to whistle to meself. I kinda bounced along, as if I didn't have a care in the world.

I'd just made it to the top of the road when I saw three fellas lounging against the wall of the local pub. They were smoking and laughing. I tried not to look at them.

Each step nearer to them increased me heart-rate. They were silent as I came alongside, only lifting themselves up a bit from the wall to stare at me as I went past. I'd just got by when I felt a stone whizz past me ear.

A guffaw of laughter.

"Brains Donnelly, off to school."

Louder laughter.

"Thinks he's somethin' special."

"Look at the poncy walk on him."

They were behind me, just at me shoulder. I kept walking, staring straight ahead.

"Hey, Billy, you queer or something?"

When I didn't answer, one of them shouted into me ear, "Well? Answer, ya little shit!"

Me ear hurt. I put me hand up to rub it and felt the burn of a cigarette. The pain shot through me hand and me stomach heaved. My legs found themselves and I ran. I ran so hard me chest hurt.

More stones were hurled at me as they ate themselves laughing.

I didn't stop running until I reached the school gates. It was the only place I felt safe. Once there, I bent over and took in huge gulps of air. Me hair was plastered to me face. When I'd got me breath back, I stood back up. I studied me hand – it didn't look too bad. Just a bit red. Hurt like hell though.

I dunno why I bothered going to school, the hassle wasn't worth it sometimes.

"In training, are you?" It was Tom. He'd come up behind me without me noticing.

"Something like that." I shoved me hand in me pocket so he wouldn't see it. I like the people in my class but I don't tell them much. They wouldn't understand. If they knew what I was like, the people I knew, they wouldn't want to talk to me anymore, so I keep meself to meself. Things are better that way.

Together Tom and me began to walk to class. "You bunked religion yesterday," he said. "Wise move."

I laughed. "Me ould fella wrote me a note." I tipped me nose. "I was sick, you know. I had to go home."

"No way?" Tom stopped walking. "Your Dad wrote you a note?"

"Yep."

"That's cool. My da would never do that for me."

I didn't answer. There were probably millions of things that his da wouldn't do that my da did. Like live in the bookies, like thump Nick up every time they rowed, like eat me ma's cooking. Writing a sick note was no big deal.

After registration, Miss Malone told me to stay behind. She made me sit in a chair beside her desk before turning and looking at me. I stared back at her from under me eyes – that way she couldn't see them. "Here," I handed her the note.

She didn't even glance at it. "I suppose your dad wrote it?" she said, all sarcastic like.

"Yeah." I couldn't help the hostile tone in me voice. "So?"

"I'm not stupid, William," she said. Her voice was soft now. Trying to make me like her. "Nick used to produce notes like that too every time he went awol."

I said nothing. Teachers hate when you stay silent.

She leaned over towards me and I shrunk back against the chair.

"Just don't start making a habit of bunking lessons," she said. "You're a great student, William, and I'd hate to see you throw it away."

I was in me arse a great student. Why do people feed you crap all the time?

"Nick wasn't like you," she went on. "He wasn't interested like you are." She produced a load of copies from her drawer and dumped them in front of her on the table. "These are the essays I asked your class to do last week, William," she said, "And your story got the top mark in the class." She took me copy out of the pile. "It's wonderful stuff."

I still said nothing. How could I write something wonderful? All it was, was a load of words about how I felt about things. Of course, I made my person in my story say the things I wanted to say, so that no one would know it was me. How could what I wanted to say be wonderful?

Bullshit.

"You've got so much to offer, William," she was at it again, using her soft voice and her nice words to win me to her side, "Don't end up like Nick."

"There's nothing wrong with Nick," I snapped back. "He's great." I stood up. I pointed to the note. "There's me note. Can I go now?"

Slowly she nodded. I could see all the bits of paper we'd fired up at her during registration clinging to her hair when she did that and I smirked a bit. "Thanks, Miss."

Out I went.

I was late for Irish. I muttered the usual apologies and slid in beside Clara. She passed her copy to me so that I could write down what they'd been doing.

"Malone chew your ear off?" she asked sympathetically.

"Yeah," I grinned at her. Then I realised I was grinning and I went red. Vicious circle.

She gave another smile at me and turned away to concentrate on the lesson.

I started to concentrate on her.

I wished it was yesterday again and she'd asked me to come out with her group. I would've been able to go. I would've had twenty quid to spend.

Still, she probably hadn't meant it and I would've made an eejit of meself.

I wanted to pluck up the nerve to say to her that I could go on Saturday if the invite was still open. I knew exactly how I should say it, what I should say. But I didn't know what she'd say and that's what held me back. I hate when I can't control what someone else is going to do, which I guess is pretty much all the time. That scares me.

I tried to think of other ways of bringing up the subject which wouldn't leave me so open. Ways that might make her ask me again. I spent Irish racking my brains thinking of how I'd do it. I don't think I wrote a single thing down for the whole lesson. In the end, I decided to go for broke. I decided to ask her out. I mean, all she could say was no.

Oh shit, all she could say was no.

After school, I still hadn't screwed up the courage. I kept starting to ask her but every time I ended up asking her for a pen or some stupid thing like that.

Then reality bit and I began to think that I was mad. I mean, what would a girl like that go out with someone like me for? She was way out of me league.

Still, I had twenty quid in me pocket and maybe that might entice her out. I was willing to settle for her liking me for me cash. I mean, it was the best thing I had going for me right then.

So after school, me hand curled around me money, I

managed to corner her. She was standing outside the sports hall waiting for her usual army of mates to walk home with.

I'll never forget the terror I felt. Not for as long as I live.

"Eh – Clara?"

"Yeah?"

Me heart jumped about a bit in me chest. I dunno if it was lust or dread.

"Eh, well, you can say no if you want." I shuffled about from foot to foot.

"What?" She was giving me a weird look. "Do you want some class notes or something?" She put up her hand and waved to someone.

Someone was coming over. My palms went sweaty.

"Well?" Clara asked, her eyes still focused on some approaching figure.

"Eh – " then, "Well, I was wonderin' – " then, "I got twenty quid, will you come out with me on Saturday?"

The minute I said it, I wanted to die.

Small silence.

"Sure."

It was only then that I realised I'd closed me eyes. I heard her say sure and I wasn't sure if it was a sure sure or a question sure. Knowing my luck it was a question sure. I nodded, still a bit afraid of looking at her. "Sure I'm sure."

I heard her laugh. I felt her give me a puck. "No," she joked. "Sure meaning yes. Yes, I'd love to head out with you on Saturday."

"Oh." I was numb. I was happy but I was numb. Gradually I let meself look at her. She was smiling at me. Full in the face. If she smiled any more I'd wither up. "That's great," I stammered. It was unbelievable, but it was great. "So I'll see you Saturday?"

"You will." She sounded as if she was amused about something.

I didn't want her to think I was a complete loss. "Around eight?"

"Fine."

"Meet you maybe outside the bowling alley and we can catch the bus into town and maybe see a film?"

"Maybe." She flashed her gorgeous smile at me. "Maybe I'd like that."

Her friend was coming closer – I could hear footsteps behind me. "Great." I wanted to go. I had to go before I said something stupid. Quit while you're ahead, that was me. "Bye so."

"See you."

I left. There was a grin on my face big enough to split it.

Chapter Nine

Smoke studied the plans. It wasn't a big room, which was good. "Cameras?" he asked.

"Here and here." A shaky finger with bitten, chewed nails pointed out the security cameras.

Smoke studied the bitten nails. This guy was a worrier. This provider of inside info was a ould one. Not exactly a great bet to have on his team. But the guy knew his stuff. That was almost all that counted.

"So end of the month's the best time to," he chose his words, "visit?"

The guy nodded. "Yeah. All the money for mortgages comes in then. The place is saturated in cash." A trembling hand began to fidget, wrestling a packet of fags from his pocket.

Smoke held out his own.

"Thanks."

The guy took a cigarette and allowed Smoke to light it for him. Once lit, he inhaled deeply. "Jesus," he breathed, "talking about this stuff makes me edgy."

Smoke remained very still. He made no comment. Edgy people were not wanted. He waited a while before resuming his questions. He needed to be sure the guy was calm enough to give the right information. After that . . . well . . . he could be done without.

Chapter Ten

Saturday couldn't come fast enough.

Or slow enough.

The whole week I was on edge, wondering if I'd done the right thing by asking Clara out. That's me – I do something, or else I don't do something and then I spend the next decade wondering if I made the right decision. Anyway, every time I saw Clara in class or talked to her, I'd know that I really liked her. Then, when I'd be at home, away from her, I'd know that she was too good for me and that I'd probably mess me big chance up. And on and on and on it went.

Me brain was twisted by the time Saturday morning came.

Saturday morning in our house is always mental. I hate weekends. Ma is always in bad form. That Saturday was no exception.

I got up around one and she was cleaning out the kitchen. When Ma cleans out the kitchen it's the worst. It's a sign that things are about to snap.

She was down on her hunkers, a basin of steaming water alongside her on the floor. Food and other stuff from the presses was scattered all over the place. To me horror, about eight massive bags of porridge were standing together in the middle of the chaos. It'd be a decade before they'd be used up. Idly I wondered why on earth she'd bought so much of the stuff.

Ma didn't look at me as I entered, only snapped out, "Fine for you able to sleep till this hour!" Then, plunging her hands into the basin, she drew out a sopping wet cloth and began to rub out the inside of the presses.

"You'll rot the wood making it so wet," I said as I went over to the kettle to flick it on. "Maybe you should squeeze out the cloth first, Ma."

That made her look at me. She rose up, her hands on her hips. She had a mad kinda look in her eye. "Well, I don't see you doing it," she barked. "Oh no, you're all talk. All talk." She shoved her face into mine and I drew back. "Just like all the other men in this kip."

"I didn't mean – "

"Bastards." She turned away from me again and squatting back down on the floor, she resumed her washing and rubbing.

Dad must've gone out to the bookies. That's probably what was wrong, I thought.

I didn't know what to do with meself. I hated leaving her there and yet I wanted to get out.

I watched as she began dumping all the food back

into the sopping wet press. Slamming the sugar-bag down into a puddle she grinned a bit as all the water began to seep into it. "That'll show him," she muttered.

Da liked sugar.

The kettle boiled. I turned and began to search for a cup.

"In the top press," Ma snapped. "I moved them."

I got two cups down and made two teas. "I made you a cup, Ma." I said it softly, so she wouldn't get angry at me. I was afraid she'd say I was wasting the tea-bags or something.

She stiffened and I braced myself. One time she'd flung hot tea at me. But only once and she hadn't meant it. It was after Da bet all his dole on a horse and we had no money for the week.

Slowly she turned around and I tried not to show that I'd seen the tear seeping down the side of her face. She came over to where I sat at the table and sat down opposite me. "Thanks, Bill," she said. "That was nice of you."

"It's all right."

"You missed breakfast," she said. "Nick ate all the porridge."

"Oh."

She took a sip of her tea. Then she said cautiously, "He seems to have a lot of money for someone who doesn't seem to be doing a lot of work."

I kept me mouth shut. No matter what I said, it'd be wrong. I badly wanted to escape.

"He even gave your father some betting money." She laughed a bit. But it wasn't a real laugh. More disbelief than anything. "He's like some kind of god, flashing all his money about."

"Yeah." I started to try and drink my tea quickly but the hotness burnt my mouth.

Ma swirled her tea about in her cup. "He's not dealing, is he?" The words jerked out of her. A fraction of silence, before she started shaking her head vigorously, as if she couldn't quite believe what she'd said. "No, I'm being stupid, of course he's not." She laughed. "I'm stupid. Imagine thinking that."

"He's not dealing, Ma."

"Well, *I* know that! Haven't I just said that? Haven't I?"

"Yeah."

"Nick'd never do something like that."

"No."

"It's cars he's working with." She nodded her head firmly. "Cars." She gripped my hand. "Isn't that right?"

"Yep." I wanted her to let my hand go, I felt as if I couldn't breathe.

She smiled an off-focus smile at me. "You're my best lad, Billy, you know that, don't you? My best lad."

I nodded.

I might be her best lad but Nick was her favourite.

I was afraid to leave her. I was afraid in case she'd have the house obliterated by the time I came back. I spent the afternoon watching her clean and wash and polish and shine. And the weird thing was that nothing looked any cleaner by the time she'd finished. I think she knew it herself and that's what made her get madder and madder.

By the time Nick and Da arrived back from the bookies, she was in the middle of doing the paintwork. Washing the paintwork, I mean.

The sound of the key in the lock made her stop. She looked at me. "Is it them?" she whispered. "Is it?"

Hope sang in her voice. She dumped the wet cloth onto the floor and made for the hall. I followed her out.

Da and Nick had just come in.

"How's the form?" Nick grinned and winked at her. He turned to me. "Only up, are you?"

I didn't answer. I felt angry at the two of them.

"Not like us." Da slung a camaraderie arm across Nick's shoulders. "Up from early, huh son?"

"Up from early," Nick grinned back.

The two laughed and Ma joined in. I hated the way she did that, thrilled now that they were back where she could keep an eye on them.

"She was worried where you were," I spoke up, hoping to help her along.

All three glared at me. "I wasn't," Ma sounded genuinely puzzled. "I never said that."

"We were only in the bookies," Nick said casually. "Just placing a few bets."

"A few *winning* bets," Da came and caught Ma by the waist. He stood behind her and kissed the top of her head. *"We're in the money. We're in the money,"* he attempted to sing.

Ma laughed again.

"A lot of money," Nick joined in. He shoved his hand into his pocket and pulled out a few tenners. He lifted them high into the air and let them float to the ground. "A lot of bloody money," he said.

Ma flapped her arms at him. "Stop that language," she said, sounding like her weekday self again. "Stop it, Nick, I'm warning you."

She giggled like a schoolgirl as he planted a kiss on her cheek.

I slipped out while they weren't paying attention.

Paul was in the garage. I was afraid that on a Saturday someone else would be working in the garage and that they wouldn't know me.

I sort of liked Paul. He wasn't like most people I met, always telling me what to do. He just accepted stuff I told him and didn't ask lots of questions. I'd been down at the garage a few nights during the week, helping him. He let me clean out the cars and polish them up. On Thursday, he even had a Corvette in for service, a big American job. He let me sit in it and I helped him do an oil change.

Today though, he just had ordinary cars, Fords and Opels and stuff.

When I arrived, Paul was sitting on an upturned oil barrel, covered in dirt and drinking tea from a huge mug.

"How's it going?" he smiled at me as I came in. "I expected you earlier. Had a gorgeous car to show you."

"Yeah?" I stood a bit away from him. I still felt awkward talking to someone as old as him. Not that he was mega-old, maybe in his thirties or something, but most of my teachers were the same age and they didn't talk to me like this guy did.

"Yep," he nodded. He indicated a cup. "Get yourself some tea if you want." He watched me as I poured meself a cup, before saying, "A roaring red Porsche."

My hand shook and tea slopped out onto my wrist. I couldn't look at him. I don't think he noticed.

"I said to myself, if Billy was here now, he'd be made up."

"Yeah." My eyes were still down.

"Such a beaut, Billy, and the noise of her."

"Yeah?"

"Pity such a cocky little prick owned her. Still, I'd be cocky if I owned one of those."

All I could see was the lovely car I'd burned. My bad feelings came back.

Paul lifted himself from the oil barrel and slapped me on the shoulder. "Right," he said, "Let's get some use outa you for the afternoon."

It was one of the best Saturday's I'd ever had. I cleaned, Paul mended and all the while he talked about different cars he'd worked on.

"There was this ould wan, right?" he said. "She drove up in this relic of a yoke one afternoon. Out she gets and

58

she tells me to give the thing a service." He looked up at me to see if I was listening. "I'm telling ya, Billy, the yoke needed more than a service. Bits of it were stuck on. She'd used superglue to get the wing-mirrors to stay in place."

"Nah!" I was grinning.

"Yep." Paul was laughing. "When she came back I told her that the best thing she could do for her car was to scrap it." He jabbed his finger at me. "An' do you know what she did?"

I shook me head.

"She went mental. Told me I didn't know what I was on about, that the car was her late husband's car, that it had sentimental value for her." Paul rolled his eyes, "Off she stormed. She gave that car door such a bang that it fell off."

I started to laugh.

"And then," Paul sucked in his breath, "she drove off minus her shaggin' door."

The two of us cracked up.

He told more stories which made me laugh. It was funny laughing. I felt weird after it, sort of lighter, more relaxed.

I left around five. Paul handed me an envelope. "Just a few quid," he said. "For helping me out."

I thought he was joking. I made no move to take it.

"You've been a great help," he said. "And you like the job. It's nothing, only a tenner, take it." Another shove of the envelope at me.

"Serious?"

"Yeah."

Slowly I took it. "Thanks." I shrugged. "I woulda done it for nothing."

Paul nodded. "Yeah, well . . . you're a good kid." He smiled. "Drop in more often, maybe a few hours every night, I need a guy who'll clean the cars after they've been serviced."

The guy was offering me a job! I couldn't believe it! "I will," I nodded vigorously. "I will."

I legged it home as fast as I could.

It hadn't been such a crap day after all.

Chapter Eleven

"It's my money too, scumbag!"

The row erupted as we were having our dinner. I couldn't eat anything because the thoughts of meeting Clara were making me feel sick.

I sat, staring at me food as Da and Nick battled it out across the table. Da was jabbing his fork about and Nick was sitting, staring at him, arms folded.

"Without me," Da pointed to himself, "you wouldn't have had a clue which horses to back." He banged his fork viciously down.

"You'll chip the table," Ma said, attempting to laugh.

"Table me arse," Da spat. "It's a fine thing when your own son cheats you out of money."

"It was my money," Nick replied. He stood up. "If I'd lost would you have paid me back?"

"Aaagh!" Da attacked his spuds.

Nick smirked. "Anyhow, Da, I gave you money this morning and you lost it." He looked at all of us. "Was that my fault? Was it?"

"Now Nick –"

"That's –"

"I have to head out now," Nick cut them short. "I'll see yez later."

I know Ma was about to ask where he was going but she stopped herself. I think she was afraid of the answer. "Bye, love," she said instead.

Da glared at his back. There was a time when he would have gone for him, but now, with Nick being so tall, he didn't do it so much anymore.

Nick sauntered out the door, whistling away to himself, and I envied him his coolness.

"Little fecker," Da muttered.

"Now, Brian," Ma said, "he did give you money. What more do you want the lad to do?"

"Oh, that's right," Da spat out. "Stick up for him. Stick up for him like you always do."

"Now, that's not fair, all I'm saying is –"

"I betcha if Billy had money, he'd let me have it, wouldn't you, Bill?"

Why did I have to get dragged into it? I gulped. "Suppose." I thought of the thirty quid in my pocket and me hand snuck involuntarily to where it was. "I guess."

"That's 'cause he's educated," Da pronounced, nodding at Ma. "A bit of schooling does no harm."

Ma shot me a look. I don't think she liked me showing Nick up. "Huh, don't forget, Nick's the one with the job, Bill's the one that costs us money."

I stared at the table and felt so ashamed.

62

I suppose I must've looked hurt or something because Ma got up and came over. Tousling my hair, she said haltingly, "But we're very proud of you, still in school and all."

I pulled my head out from under her hand.

Sometimes I hated Nick.

I was at the bowler five minutes early. I looked all right, I suppose. Nick had gone out, so I'd borrowed his Nike trainers. Even though I'm shorter than him, we both have the same shoe size. Nick says that that means I'm going to be as tall as him. I hope so. Girls go for tall fellas.

The bowler was doing great business, piles of people were going into it. Every time someone passed me I'd think it was Clara and when it wasn't I'd feel a bit panicky and relieved all at the same time. I lit a fag to calm meself down.

I was on me second fag when she arrived. She'd done something to her hair, I dunno what, but it was all shiny and silky-looking. She had nice clothes on too – a short skirt that made me suck me breath in. I wondered for the millionth time why the hell she was going out with me. "Hiya." She even gave me a smile.

I nodded and blew out a stream of smoke. I was afraid to speak in case me voice shook. I threw the cigarette on the ground and stamped it out.

We stood, looking at each other.

I guessed it was up to me. "Where to?" I asked.

She shrugged. "I don't mind. Anywhere you like."
Another smile.

I'd memorised the times of all the films in all the cinemas. "We can go to the square and catch a film – maybe?"

"Right."

"OK." I turned and started to walk to the bus stop. Me mind was blank and full of stupid stuff all at the one time. I didn't know what to say to her now that I had her on her own. And 'cause I was so bloody nervous, I walked too fast – soon she was running to catch up. "Sorry," I said, slowing down.

"It's all right."

We walked side by side to the bus stop.

I took out another fag and offered her one.

"No."

So I smoked while she stood beside me.

When I finished, I lit another one. I had to do something with me hands. "Clara?" I held out the packet to her.

"No."

Now there was a pissed-off edge in her voice. Great! I stared ahead, puffing for dear life on me fag.

"Billy," Clara said haltingly. "Are you sorry you asked me out now?"

"What?" I got such a shock, I ended up exhaling straight into her face.

After she'd stopped coughing and choking and I'd stopped apologising and blushing, she said, "Well? Are you sorry you asked me out?" Suddenly she didn't look

64

so friendly anymore. "I mean, let's get this straight, it was you that asked me out."

I didn't know what she was on about. "Sorry?"

"What is going on here?" Her voice had risen a little and a few people turned to look.

I wanted to puke with nerves. I shoulda listened to the voice of reason. The voice that told me there was no way this was going to work out. "Clara –"

"What are you playing at?"

I was dying. What had I done? What did she want? "Nothing," I shook me head. "I'm not playin' at anything?"

"So what's the problem?"

She was waiting on an answer I didn't have. "What? Sorry?"

"Do you not want to go out now, is that it?"

"What?"

"Jesus!" She folded her arms and shook her head and looked at me.

Now more people were staring.

"I – I –" I started to speak. Then I realised that I didn't know what I was about to say. Then I thought that I just couldn't blow it. Then I knew that being me, I'd blow it anyhow. Then I blurted out, "Have I made you mad?"

She gazed incredulously at me.

Someone laughed.

I was going to wreck things if I didn't say something. But I didn't know what to say. "I want to go out with you," I said. I think this was what she wanted to hear, so I went on, "I like you."

She seemed to relax a bit. "So why aren't you talking to me?" she asked. "I mean we get on great in school."

Oh God! This was scary. "Wasn't I talking?" I said. "Sorry." I held out me hand. I didn't think about it, just did it. To my amazement, she took me hand and squeezed it. It felt nice. "So," I said, determined to say something, "eh – how was your Saturday then?"

That was all I had to do. Like in school, she was off, chatting away. Making me smile. So I told her a bit about Paul and the garage and suddenly it was easy to be with her. I never wanted the bus to come.

I let her choose the film. It was a stupid one, all about someone falling in love with someone who loved someone else. I didn't care, I liked to look at her watching it. I wanted everyone to know I was with her, so sometime around the middle of the film, I put me arm on her shoulder and pulled her to me. She turned her face up to mine and, on impulse, I bent me head and kissed her.

She put her hand up to me face and rubbed me cheek.

I could have spent the rest of the time snogging her but I guess she wanted to see the film. She turned away, after giving me another million-watt smile. And I couldn't take me eyes off her face.

I had kissed Clara Daly.

We went to McDonald's afterwards. It was my idea. I still had a pile of cash left and I decided that I might as well show her a good time. Maybe if I did, she might like me even more. Carrying our Big Macs and chips we found a table and sat down.

"That was a great film," Clara said as she opened her burger and began taking out all the gherkin bits. "Thanks."

I indicated her gherkin. "Can I have those?" When she nodded, I opened me own burger and began stuffing them into it. "I love them and I'm starving." I took a huge bite out of the Big Mac, almost eating the whole lot in one go. Then I wondered if she thought I looked like a pig, eating like that. Ma said I was a pig when I ate. But Clara didn't seem to mind – she was grinning at me.

She had her chin cupped in her hand and she was smiling. "Did you not eat a dinner or something?" Before I answered, she said, "I couldn't, I was so nervous about tonight."

Suddenly, some of me burger went down the wrong way. I started to cough and choke. Tears started coming out of me eyes. Clara shoved the Coke at me. I took a gulp and me whole throat hurt as the huge pile of food tried to ram itself down. But I couldn't spit it out. So I braved it.

Clara was looking anxiously at me. "Are you all right?"

I grinned. "Did you say you were nervous about going out with me?" I wanted to hear her say it again.

She blushed. Staring at her chips she nodded. "Yeah."

"Why?" The disbelief in me voice made her look up. "Why?" I asked again.

She gave a shrug. As if she was embarrassed. "Well, you know, I thought you'd think I was boring."

Hang on here, I thought to meself. "Boring?" I said.

Another shrug.

This was the girl I'd had dreams about for the past year. "I've fancied you for ages," I said. I felt I could say that. I knew she wouldn't laugh now. "I just, well, I didn't think you'd be seen dead with me." That was the hard part to say.

Clara looked at me. Her eyes sparkled, as if I'd just said something brilliant. "Really?"

"Yeah." I started to tear me big Mac box up.

"It's just, you know," Clara made a face. "You're so laid-back and cool in school. I'm sort of a swot really." She gave a laugh. "I was convinced you used to laugh at me behind my back."

I was laid-back and cool? What planet was the girl on? Still, her saying it made me feel really cool. It made me brave enough to take her hand. I was going to tell her that I'd never laugh at her, but it sounded so crappy and corny and slushy. So I said, "You ready to go?"

Yeah, I know, dead romantic.

I walked her home. Her house was really nice on the outside. Big would describe it best. Her front garden was the size of our back and front garden doubled.

"Nice gaff," I said.

She turned towards me and I took her two hands in mine. We stood, looking at each other. She squeezed me hands and I bent my forehead so it was touching hers. "Want to go out again sometime?" I asked. I hadn't planned on doing that. It just came out.

"Sometime would be great," she agreed.

I swallowed hard. Did that mean she didn't want to see me again? Then I remembered that I was laid-back and cool. "Sometime soon?"

"Fine." There was a smile on her face.

"Like maybe tomorrow?"

"Afternoon?"

"Done."

She laughed. "Call for me around three, all right?"

"Here?" My coolness deserted me. She might like me but I doubted that her parents would.

"Here," she nodded.

I didn't know what to say. I didn't want to let her down. "Fine," I said eventually. I didn't know whether to kiss her or not. It wasn't that I was a novice or anything, it was just that I'd never actually gone out with anyone on a date before. Seeing girls was one thing, going out was new to me. I think she was waiting to be kissed though. So I kissed her and she kissed me back.

It was like fireworks in me.

"See you so," I said, letting her go. I was convinced I'd seen someone watching us from her house.

"Yeah," she nodded. "See you, Billy." She blew me a kiss as I left.

I didn't turn around to see her go in. I just walked away. That was the laid-back thing to do, right?

Chapter Twelve

Gathered around the table. Smoke watching as they studied the plans. Whiteser calmly pointing out all the routes away from the job. Discussions. Ideas. Brainstorming. Fart coming up with some great stuff.

Smoke observed them all. Whiteser was calm. Icily so. He was always like that about jobs. Johnny was silent, head in his hands absorbing every word. Smoke knew Johnny was thinking about the guns. Johnny liked guns. Johnny was thrown out of the army because he liked guns too much. Smoke blessed the day they'd found Johnny. Then last but not least, Fart. Aptly named. The guy had a backside like a sewer. Irritable bowel, he called it. Smelly bowel Whiteser called it behind his back. But Fart was brilliant. A master planner. Smoke came up with the hits, Fart came up with the planning. A good team.

In fact that was what was so brilliant about everything Smoke did. Teamwork. No outsiders. Nick would be the latest edition to the gang. Smoke savoured the thoughts of Nick before tuning back in to the discussions.

Fart was asking about the car. His whiskey and smoke voice, barely rising above a whisper. "Donnelly?" he asked.

Whiteser nodded. "I met him this evening. He knows what we want. I gave him the keys to the lock- up." Staring over at Smoke, he said, "He's driving on the day."

Fart looked at Smoke. "Is he good?"

Smoke resented the comment. He didn't reply, just looked the other way.

"He's good," Johnny confirmed. "He's cool too. Won't panic."

"Good."

Smoke passed around the cigars. Three more weeks to go.

Chapter Thirteen

Sunday morning, sun pouring in through the window, slanting across the floor and burning open me eyelids. Nick was sitting cross-legged on his bed, his back to me, staring out the window. His shoulders were hunched up, his elbows rested on the windowsill. I don't think in the whole of me life, I've ever seen Nick sit so still for so long. For some reason, the light feelings in me began to seep away.

I closed me eyes against the dread that I felt.

Nick musta heard me move or maybe he just wanted to wake me up. "Oy, Bill," he said in a loud whisper. "You awake?"

"No." I buried my head underneath the covers. I wanted to fill my head with thoughts of last night.

I heard Nick jumping off his bed and coming over. "Listen, d'you fancy coming out this afternoon. I've got a heap of dough to spend." I could tell he was smiling.

"No can do."

"Sure you can," Nick started to shake me. "Sure what

else would you be doing?" He sat down on the bed. "I just fancy having a bit of a mental time. We can head off to Bray on the dart and play on the slots. Or maybe the video games." He waited for me to say something.

"Go with someone else," I said.

There was a stunned silence.

"It's just . . ." I stopped, took a breath, "I'm going out meself this afternoon."

"Yeah?"

"Yeah." Back down under the covers again. That was as much as I wanted to admit.

"With some of the lads from school or something?"

I felt a bit annoyed at the disbelief in his voice. Just 'cause I didn't have loadsa friends like him. Though he never said people were his friends. They were just people he knew, he said.

"It's with a girl – right." That shook him. He went a bit pale. I grinned. "See, I do have some pulling power."

Nick didn't say anything for a bit. Then he said softly, "D'you really like this girl?" He was staring at me and making me feel stupid and annoyed.

"No," I said, as if he was dumb. "Dawww."

He didn't even smile. Just closed his eyes and said "Jesus" or something like that. Then he turned back to me. "Billy, what've I told you about having ties? You – can't – have – ties."

"What?" I laughed.

"Break it off with her." He looked hard at me. "If you like her, dump her."

He was serious. I couldn't believe it. "No way," I shook my head. "You can't tell me to do that." Screwing up my courage, because I didn't like fighting or going against Nick, I said, "Anyhow, it's none of your business."

"Billy, you don't understand . . ." his voice faltered. He stopped and lifted himself up from the bed. "Aw, what the hell," he shrugged. "Do what you want."

I watched him walk out of the room. I pushed what he'd said out of my head. What's the words of the Simon and Garfunkel song? A man hears what he wants to hear or something like that?

That's me.

All over.

I surfaced around one.

Da was in the kitchen, chatting away to Ma. He was painstakingly reading the racing results and she was bent over the frying-pan torturing some other harmless piece of food.

"Sleep well, did you?" Ma joked. There wasn't the sarcasm of yesterday in her remarks. With Da and Nick at home, she was as happy as she could be.

"All right," I said.

"There's tea in the pot." Da pointed over to where the teapot stood on the cooker. "I just made some."

"And lunch'll be ready in a tick," Ma gave the pan a shake. "I just fried up some rice for you."

"Lovely jubbley," Da rubbed his hands in eager anticipation.

"Get your brother, will you?" Ma asked me. "He's in the front room sulking over something or other. He's had a face on him all morning."

Nick was sitting, flicking through the pages of a car manual. I think he must've lifted it 'cause it looked like it cost about thirty quid. He looked up as I poked me head around the front-room door.

"Lunch," I said.

"Thanks." Standing up from the chair he gave a stretch. I was about to leave when he stopped me with, "Hang on, Bill."

"Yeah?"

He looked sheepishly at me. "I'm sorry about this morning, I guess the way I do things can't be the same as the way you do things."

"Yeah." I smiled at him.

"So maybe, when you've finished with this young wan today, you'll come out with me tonight?" He looked hopefully at me.

I dunno why he was so anxious for me to go with him.

"I just feel like spending money on *us*," Nick said. He gazed at the carpet. "Like the lads are fine, but like, half the time they don't want to know me when I'm broke. And the ould fella only gives me the time of day when I've a few quid to give him." He sounded sad at that. Still, he smiled at me when he said, "So, now that I've cash, I say to hell with them. I don't need them. See what I mean?"

"Yeah." I saw what he meant. I believed it too. Without money you were nothing.

"So Bray tonight?"

"Yeah."

After lunch I walked to Clara's. Nick let me borrow his trainers again. He woulda lent me his new shirt that he bought but it was massive on me. There was a terrible smell of garlic off me, even though I'd changed me clothes after lunch and everything. Ma had put about a million cloves of garlic into her fried rice. The smell was all over the house. Vampires would've been killed on the moon with the stench.

Still, I reckoned that Clara wouldn't mind. I had a tenner in me pocket so at least I'd be able to bring her somewhere.

I arrived at her gaff around three. For some thick reason, I thought she'd be looking out the window for me and that when she saw me she'd come out. No such luck. I ended up walking by her house about ten times before making the brave decision to ring the door-bell.

Up the garden path, I thought everyone was looking at me. It was like I was exposed or something. The sound of her doorbell seemed to fill up the whole street. Me hands were sweating, me heart was banging and I badly needed a fag. But I'd smoked so many last night that they were gone.

I could see someone coming to the door and I hoped like mad that it'd be Clara. But, like every other time in me life, me hopes were smashed. It was Clara's ma.

She looked all right, for a ma, I guess. The usual cagey eyes, the forced smile. "Hello?" She kept her hand on the door.

"Eh, hi," I stammered. "Is, eh, is Clara in?"

"Yeah," she opened the door wider. "She's looking at the telly. Go on in to her."

I couldn't. I couldn't go in. "Eh, no," I said. I rubbed me hands down me jeans. "Eh, can you just tell her Billy called."

She gave a laugh. I wanted to glower at her, but I couldn't – she *was* Clara's ma. "We don't bite," she said, as if everything was a big joke. "Come on."

"Is that you, Billy?" Clara's voice. I smiled in relief as she came out into the hallway. "I'm just watching the end of a film on the telly, come on in for a sec."

"I'm after asking him already," her ma said, walking away.

Then it was just me and her. She held out her hand to pull me into the house but I didn't take it. "Come out," I said, nodding towards the gate. "I'll buy you something to eat."

She gave me a funny look.

"Please?"

"Oh, all right," she grinned. "Seeing as it's you."

I liked the way she said that. As if she was only doing it 'cause it was me. As if I was special to her or something.

I waited on the step while she got her coat. "Bye Mam, I'm heading out," she yelled, before slamming the front door and, as natural as anything, taking my hand in hers.

"So what's the plan?" she asked as we began to walk.

I shrugged. "We can grab a bite to eat, I'm starving."

"You seem to be always starving!"

"Yeah, well . . ."

"I mean you must be just after your dinner, I can smell garlic off you."

I didn't say anything to that.

"I love the smell of garlic."

"You should pay a visit to our house so," I said dryly. I hadn't meant to, the less said about my gaff the better.

"And you should pay a visit to ours." She was looking up into me face. She tugged on me hand. "Why wouldn't you come in?" she asked, really soft.

I turned away from her. "No reason, I just wanted to have you on me own."

I don't know if she believed me or not – I don't see why she shouldn't have, it was partly the truth – but she let the subject drop. Instead she squeezed my hand even harder and laughed.

The fact that I made her laugh made me feel good.

We went to McDonald's again. She just had a coffee while I ate chips, a Big Mac and one of them apple-tart yokes they sell. I offered her some of me chips but she didn't want any.

"I'm too fat."

"Are you?" I looked at her, feeling puzzled. I didn't think she was fat at all.

For some reason, she sorta looked surprised. Then

78

she looked offended. Then she gave a smile and rolled her eyes. "You're mad, you," she said for no reason. Then she reached over and took about nearly half me bleedin' chips. I had to buy another load.

After that, we walked. I'm not big into walking but with her it was nice. I can't even remember what we talked about, probably nothing much.

I think I bored her stupid by pointing out any nice cars I saw. It's the only thing I know about and I guess I had to impress her some way.

"What would you say," I said, "if one day I came up to your house with a car?"

That's me dream, to have a car of me own. One I can go wherever I want to in.

Clara looked at me. "I don't know," she giggled. "What a mad question!"

"Naw, seriously," I said, grinning at her. "Would you be impressed like?"

She shrugged. "Oh yeah," she said, sort of mocking. "Really impressed."

I felt hurt.

"You don't need a car to impress me," she said.

Right, I felt like saying.

"Or cash," she said.

I nearly laughed out loud.

"Just you is good enough."

Her kiss on me lips was the only thing that stopped me from laughing into her face.

Chapter Fourteen

I was sorry I'd agreed to go out with Nick. Being with Clara was great. It was like she made me forget where I came from and she made everything seem easier somehow.

And harder too. It was hard to be with her and still be meself.

With Nick, at least, I felt he understood me.

He was waiting outside the house when I got back. Well, he was cowering in the bushes in our overgrown garden. "Billy," he whispered, "Don't go in."

He was like something from *'Allo 'Allo* as he came out from the bush, totally covered in muck. He put his finger to his lips and dragged me away from the house. "You don't want to go in," he said urgently. "Ma's making cheese-balls."

He was right. I didn't want to go in. "Christ," I said, "you just saved me stomach from acid overload."

"I'm not Christ," Nick said, brushing himself down, "but thanks for the compliment."

Laughing, we legged it across the road, over the green and to the bus stop. I felt a bit guilty at not turning up for dinner but cheese-balls were the pits. They hadn't even the distinction of being a real recipe, just something me ma concocted from time to time. They consisted of cheese and some really strange herbs, all melted and rolled into balls. Every time I ate them, I was awful sick.

We didn't have to wait long for the bus and, after Nick paid our fares, we climbed upstairs and sat in the very front.

"Fag?" Nick held out his packet to me.

I took one and we lit up.

You're not allowed to smoke on buses now but no one ever says anything. It's cool, so it is, smoking away and everyone giving you dirty looks and whispering about you. It makes me feel really great, so it does.

Nick lay back in the seat and put his feet on the sill in front. "So how was the big date then?" he asked.

I nodded. "All right."

"You sleeping with her?"

I have to say, 'cause I'm being honest here writing this, that I felt a bit annoyed. For Clara more than for me. "None of your business," I snapped.

Nick laughed. "You're not so." His eyes sparkled at me. "She a bit shy then?"

I felt like telling him that Clara wasn't the sort of girl that he knew, that she didn't just go shagging every fella she met, but I couldn't. Nick wouldn't understand that. "A bit," I conceded.

"Hate that." Nick blew a long stream of smoke down his nose. "I never bother with shy girls." He poked me in the belly. "Not worth the trouble."

I didn't bother replying. *He* wasn't worth the trouble.

We got to Bray around eight. The place was buzzing as it was coming into the summer. The smell of chips and vinegar was everywhere. We ate two singles as we walked along the promenade. The lights and noise and laughter made me dizzy. It was a great place to be in.

We finished eating and, after tossing our chip bags away, Nick took me arm and dragged me into the nearest arcade.

"Here," he said, pulling a twenty spot from his pocket, "take that and do what you want."

"And what are you doing?" I asked. I'd thought we were going to be hanging out together.

"Just playing the slots."

He sounded a bit like Da when he said that, so I couldn't look him in the face. "Fine," I said. "See you in a bit."

I walked around the place, not sure exactly what I did want to do. In the end, I decided to spend a tenner and keep the rest to bring Clara out again.

I had a great night playing the video games. There's this brilliant one, where it's like you're driving a Grand Prix car. You can sit into it and everything. I got the highest score. It was a sinch. Nick says one day I'll be as good a driver as him.

When me tenner was gone, I went in search of me brother. He was sitting in front of the slots, with a flower-pot full of cash in his hand. Most of it was gone. I dunno what was so brilliant about pushing a button and watching things whirl about.

"Be with you in a sec," Nick said. He didn't take his eyes off the machine.

After about another hour, he was smashed broke. Nothing left except our bus-fares home.

I suppose he wasn't really like Da. If he had been, he would've shoved our bus-fares into the slots as well.

But he didn't.

We caught a bus back to the city centre and then stood in town waiting on another bus to bring us back home. To be honest I couldn't wait to get back. Nick was in shit form. He kept going on and on about odds and the way the slots were fixed and I just couldn't take much more.

"See, Bill," he said as the bus drove up, "every so many times you win." He looked baffled. "How come I didn't? How come – huh?"

"I dunno, Nick," I said. I watched the bus-driver do the usual bus-driver shit-arse thing they love doing. Getting off the bus and saying to all us eejits, shivering in the night air, that he'd be back in a sec.

"Asshole," I commented.

"What?" Nick, realising that I wasn't listening to him, turned to look at what I was giving out about. "Oh yeah," he said in agreement. Then, quite suddenly he laughed. "Let's take it." He gave me a nudge. "Come on, Bill, ever driven a bus before?"

He had that look on his face. The one that means he's doing it anyhow.

"Jesus, Nick – " I gulped. "We can't . . ."

"Watch me," Nick backed away from me, hands in the air, smiling. "Watch this, Billy boy."

He turned and sauntered casually over to the bus, pushed the button and the doors opened. "Coming?" he asked.

Everyone in the queue was gawking. Fearfully looking at me brother.

I wanted to be part of it.

"Sure," I ran up beside him. Me heart was hammering but adrenaline was pumping. I jumped onto the bus.

Nick did a real cool-looking jump into the driver's seat. It was no prob, the thick had left everything unlocked, keys in the ignition, everything.

"Hey, you can't . . ." one ould fella protested, coming up as far as the door.

Nick gave him the two fingers and, finding the button to close the door, almost took the guy's nose off his face.

"Bye, suckers!" Nick said turning the key and sparking the bus into life.

I couldn't stop laughing.

Nick drove the bus as if it was the Porsche. He turned the radio up real loud and the sound made the whole machine vibrate. One of the songs that came on was

Summer Holiday and that cracked us both up. We pelted along singing the words at the top of our voices.

I didn't know where we were headed until we came to a roundabout and a big sign announced that the M50 was straight ahead.

"No way!" I breathed.

"Not no way," Nick joked. "Motorway!"

And onto the motorway we went.

He drove in the outside lane at what felt like a hundred miles an hour – though I guess it couldn't have been. Still, those babies can move.

"Hiya luv!" Nick took both hands off the steering wheel to wave at some young wan in a car staring away at us. The bus zig-zagged a bit but that only made us laugh louder.

Any car that we passed, Nick would flash the big beams of the bus at them and they'd gawk and point at us.

"That shows 'em," Nick winked at me. "Don't mess with the Donnelly brothers."

I liked the sound of that.

Of course it wasn't long before we heard it. Even above the sound of the radio we heard it. Police siren. Coming behind us but getting closer.

I was so high at that stage, I don't think I cared about being caught. I don't think Nick gave a damn either but his hands tightened on the steering wheel. "Think you can drive huh?" he muttered. "I'll show yez."

More acceleration. This time, though, he swerved off

the motorway up a slip road. It made him slow down.
"Now!" he screamed at me. "Now!"

I looked at him.

"Get off, Billy!" he screamed. "I'm slowing down,
get off."

The doors of the bus opened. I stared at him. "I can't
get off," I said, confused. "No way."

Nick put his foot down and the bus jerked to a
complete halt. A car almost smashed into us. The driver
blasted his horn but we both ignored it.

"Either you get off or we both get done," Nick said
savagely. "And I will get done, you know that." He was
still on probation from last time.

I stared at him. "I can't leave you."

"Billy, will you move it!" he yelled. He turned
panicky eyes behind him. "Come on."

"Why?"

"'Cause I don't want you getting caught with me, all
right?" Nick bit his lip. "You're me brother, but, like,
you don't want to get caught. All right?"

In that moment, I knew I loved him more than anyone
else on this earth.

I jumped off.

I ran up the verge and hid, lying down flat.

The lights in front went green and Nick took off. The
cop cars arrived about twenty seconds later.

I stayed there all night.

I was afraid to go home.

I was afraid to find out what happened.

Part Two

One week later

Chapter Fifteen

It was on the front page of the local paper and a small piece even appeared in the middle pages of *The Irish Independant*.

"Bail Refused for Bus Bandit" was the caption of the *South Leader*. Pictures of Nick, looking mean and ugly, sneered at us as we ate our breakfast.

I couldn't eat. I don't think I'd eaten anything all week. I hadn't even gone outside the door all week, just spent time up in me room feeling sick and guilty. I couldn't face anyone. Nick had been great in court, swearing blind that he'd been the only one on the bus even though others said there had been two people. Nothing could be proved because just before he'd been caught, he'd smashed the on-board security camera and tape.

I wanted to tell everyone I had been with him but I knew Nick would've gone mental, so I kept me mouth shut.

The only day I had gone out was to see Nick in court. The judge, the fecker, had refused bail on the grounds that Nick was likely to re-offend if released.

The picture in the paper didn't capture the look of panic on me brother's face when the judge had said that, or the way Nick had shrugged hopelessly at the three of us. And mouthed "sorry" over to Ma. No, they'd photographed him at his worst.

Ma was busy turning the pages. She'd been hoovering and cleaning and crying all week. She hadn't even bothered waking me for school any day, just let me stay in bed, which was fine by me.

She stopped at a picture, taken of her as she emerged from the courtroom, and studied it. "That's an awful one of me," she exclaimed, starting to blubber again. She held it out to Da. "Brian, isn't that an awful one of me?"

"Desperate," he agreed.

"I thought I looked nice yesterday." She took a deep breath and continued, "I wore the best stuff I had. That solicitor chap, he said to look respectable."

"I thought you looked gorgeous," Da patted her on the hand and she smiled. Then, looking at the picture of Nick, Da shook his head. "How could he get sent down?" he scoffed. "He even had the best bloody lawyer, all paid for by his mates and still . . ."

"He always had good friends," Ma sniffed.

I didn't say anything.

I picked up me bag. I didn't want to think about

Nick's friends. It didn't add up. Nick said that they only wanted him when he had money – why the hell would they pay for a lawyer for him?

"I suppose you've nothing to say in his defence?" The way Ma snapped at me made me jump. She began clearing off the table.

I ignored her.

"All he did was take a bloody bus, for God's sake. It was just a prank."

"Yeah." The guilt was killing me. "I'll see yez later."

Ma dropped the dishes wholesale into the sink. There was a breaking, smashing sound. "Just go to school," she shouted. "I suppose you're delighted he's stuck in there."

I flinched at the tone in her voice. "No."

There was silence. Da got slowly up from the table and put his arm about Ma's shoulders. He kissed her gently on the head. "Go on," he said to me. "Get ready for school. She's just upset."

"Sorry, Ma."

She waved me away and buried her head further into Da's chest.

I studied the two of them. Da was being really good since Nick had been banged up, being nice to Ma, hardly going out at all. In fact, I think he was glad that Nick was out of the way, I dunno why, but I got that impression from him. Anyhow, him being good didn't seem to cut any ice with Ma. She was totally miserable over the whole thing.

"Will you stop standing there and go to school," Ma yelled. "Just get out."

I picked up me schoolbag and left.

The minute I walked into class that morning, I knew they all knew. I came in the door and the whole room fell silent. Some people stared at me and then, realising that they were staring, turned away, trying to pick up the threads of their conversations.

"Hi, Bill," Tom said as I sat in beside him. "How's the form?"

He stared at me, looking concerned.

I shrugged.

Then I don't think he knew what to say so he just nodded.

I didn't want to talk to anyone – in fact, I didn't want to even be in school but I had nowhere else to go. Home wasn't an option as Nick wasn't there. The only place was the garage and Paul wouldn't let me work if he thought I was bunking school. I had to fill me mind with something. Like it or not, school was me best bet.

I didn't notice Clara come in. The first I saw of her was when she sat herself down beside me. Meeting her was what I dreaded. I didn't want it to be over with her.

"Hi," she said.

"Hello." I stared at the desk and braced meself. I wondered would she wait 'til after school to call it off.

"Why didn't you contact me all week?" she asked, in a really low voice so that no one else would hear.

The question surprised me. I looked at her and, not for

the first time, me heart lurching made me feel sick. "I didn't think . . ." I shrugged. "Well, I dunno. I guess I thought you wouldn't want to know me."

Her eyes widened. "Why?" She looked really puzzled.

Was the girl stupid? "'Cause of Nick and all the trouble I am." The words came out sounding harsh. She winced a bit, so I tried to say something to make her understand. "You don't want to be hanging around with me," I said. "I mean, you could have anyone."

Voiced. My deepest fear. *She* could have anyone.

"I don't want anyone else," she said. She took my hand. "Just you."

I'm not a touching person, especially in public. But her hand in mine was like adrenaline.

"What your brother does is nothing to do with us," she went on.

I wondered if me being on the bus would've made a difference to what she thought . . . but she'd never know. And besides, I'd never do anything like it again.

"All right?" She quirked her eyebrows.

"Yeah." It was the first time I'd grinned all week.

After school I went to the garage. I couldn't face going home. Paul didn't know anything about Nick or the bus. Well, maybe he did, but he didn't know I was Nick's brother and I wasn't going to tell him.

"Haven't seen you in a while," he grinned at me. "What happened, you go mad on the tenner I gave you or what?"

"Or what," I answered.

Paul laughed and left it at that. That's why he was so cool – he didn't ask weird nosey questions.

"Where the hell were you?" Ma barked, swivelling around to stare at me as I opened the back door.

"Just walkin'."

"It's 6.30 now – school finished two hours ago. Where did you go?"

"Just around."

She glared at me. Pointing towards the frying-pan, she snapped, "Your dinner's in there and you needn't blame me if it's ruined."

"It'll be ruined anyway," I mumbled.

"What's that? What did you say?"

Ignoring her, I took the lid off the pan. Smoke billowed out. I wondered what this dinner was meant to be.

"It's stew," Ma said. She got a plate from the press. "Here, stick it on that."

I dumped the contents of the pan onto the plate. "Thanks."

She sat down opposite me as I began to eat.

"Just walking? That's all you did?" Her face was sort've under mine, as if she was trying to look into me eyes. She sounded angry and anxious.

"Yeah, felt like a walk."

"How was school?"

"It was all right."

"Good." She patted me arm. "Good," she repeated.

There was silence. She broke it as she got up from the table. "I'll leave you to it," she said, indicating the dinner. "I'll just go in to your Dad."

"Sure." I watched her leave, then I emptied the rest of me dinner into the sink and washed it away down the drain.

Chapter Sixteen

Smoke didn't move. Sitting upright, eyes wide. Whiteser sat opposite him and remained like that for twenty minutes while Smoke decided what he wanted to say and how to say it.

"Three weeks to go," Smoke said.

Whiteser gulped. Smoke was talking quietly. Smoke talked like that when he was dangerously close to the edge.

"Three weeks and what happens?"

It wasn't a question Whiteser wanted to answer.

Smoke pointed a finger at him. "You pay Donnelly a visit. You pay him a visit and tell him how I'm feeling." He flicked his eyes to somewhere over Whiteser's shoulder. "You tell him he really messed up big time. You tell him he better sort this out before we sort things out."

Whiteser gulped. "Is there no other driver we can get?"

"That's what Nick's going to tell you, isn't it?" Smoke said.

"Yeah." Whiteser stood up. "Right."

Smoke watched him leave. It was hard to keep calm when things were so bad, but if he could contain his rage until he could control it, he'd be on top. Years building up a team for this job, years planning, years watching and waiting to find the right people. No outsiders could be considered now, not now . . . his rage grew and he bit his lip to clamp it down. He wondered if Donnelly would be able to contain fear as good. For years he had watched that kid, taken pride in him from a distance and now . . . he'd pay. He would. Smoke knew how to make people pay.

Chapter Seventeen

There was mad excitement this morning. The three of us headed off to the prison to visit Nick. The whole thing seemed to cheer Ma up. She'd been really down all week. Not that she acted down – she'd spent the week in manic activity. Dusting, hoovering, washing. It was just that she kept crying on and off the whole time. Da said it was her hormones. But I didn't think so.

The visit seemed to make her come to life again. She'd even put a red colour in her hair. "I can't let my son down," she'd said.

"You look like your head's on fire," Da had remarked sourly.

She refused to talk to him the whole journey to the prison.

I sat between them on the bus, feeling stupid because anything Da said, Ma sniffed at.

Just before we got to the gates, Ma went white. She put her hand into mine and Da's and said tearfully, "Oh, I hope he's all right."

Da shrugged.

"I hope they're feeding him all right."

She didn't understand why I laughed. She gave me a belt around the head. "It's no laughing matter," she snapped. "It's your brother you're visiting and don't you forget it."

"I don't think we could," Da said airily. "I mean, even his name would remind us of where he is."

"Oh God!" Ma shrieked as Da chortled at his wit. "Oh God." She dropped both our hands and marched ahead.

Da winked at me and ran to catch her up.

They still weren't talking by the time Nick was led down to see us. We sat on one side of a table and he sat at the other.

Other prisoners were there, chatting away to people they knew. The place seemed all right, a bit like a Housing Office in the council.

"It's not as horrible as I expected," Ma said in a big loud whisper.

I was about to say something when I saw Nick being led in. He didn't look like Nick. His head was down and his shoulders had a kind of slope to them. He walked slow too, not bouncy like usual.

"Nick," Ma jumped up to hug him.

She stopped in mid-air, which looked kinda funny. Her arms outstretched as if she was going to stop herself from falling over. "Nick!" she said again, totally differently.

Nick had a huge black eye. His lip was swollen too.

"Ma." He attempted a smile as he slid into his seat.

The three of us gaped at him.

"Oh Nick," Ma's voice sounded wobbly and high. I think she was about to cry.

"What happened?" I asked. I couldn't take me eyes from his face.

"Obvious, isn't it?" Da spoke up. "Some queer tried it on, did they, son?"

Da's voice seemed to rise above everyone's.

Ma's shriek did rise above everyone's.

I wanted to die.

Nick, however, gave a splutter of laughter. "Naw."

Relief. Relief. Relief.

"I, eh . . ." Nick's grin slid from his face. "I slipped on me way to breakfast. Fell down some stairs."

"There now," Ma gave Da a wallop. "Making a big deal about things." She reached out and ran her fingers gently down Nick's face. "Is it sore, pet?"

I was horrified to see the tears glisten in his eyes. Quick as anything, he turned away. "Naw," he shrugged. "Naw."

The guilt I felt began once again to eat at me. It was all I could think of as Da began asking questions on queer policies and Ma began asking him how well he was eating and had he made any friends.

Nick answered everything blandly, not giving too much away, but I don't think they noticed.

Just before we left, he said, "Listen guys, d'you mind if I just have a word with Bill on his own?"

Ma and Da looked stunned.

"About what?" Ma sounded offended.

"Just about school," Nick gave an embarrassed shrug, "I'm in school here and I want to ask his advice on what to study."

"Boring!" Da pronounced. He stood up. "Come on Mayro, let's go."

Ma shook him off. "It better be about school," she said. She surprised me by touching me on the shoulder. "Billy's a good lad." A squeeze, which left me staring stupefied after her. I wished she'd do it again.

"Bill." Nick's urgent-sounding voice broke in on me thoughts. I turned to him. "Listen, Bill, I'm in deep shit."

I didn't want to hear. Nick and deep shit sounded bad.

Nick closed his eyes. "Listen, some guys are really mad at me, I can't tell you everything but please, take care, right?"

"Nick?"

Nick put his finger to his lips. His eyes looked half crazed. "That girl you were seeing?"

"What?"

"Break it off with her," he ordered.

I opened me mouth to say something but he cut me short. "Do it, Bill." He stood up. "Please?"

Then he walked away from me.

Chapter Eighteen

I couldn't do it though.

Clara and me were sitting in her kitchen. She'd just made me a huge mug of coffee and dumped a tin of biscuits on the table in front of me.

"Eat up," she ordered, grinning. "It'll mean less for me and Mam, so we won't put on weight."

Saying that, she took two chocolate digestives and began to munch.

Isn't it awful in someone's house, trying to find your way into a packet of biscuits without making any rustling sounds? And then, trying to eat and talk at the same time? I hate it. But it was just me and her, so I guess it wasn't as bad as it could have been. I'd actually plucked up the courage to go into her house, which was a major achievement for me. Well, I didn't want to go breaking it off with her on the street.

Only I couldn't break it off.

She had her legs tucked up under her and was curled

up into her seat. She looked so, I dunno, so innocent or something. "So tell us," she said, "How's your brother?"

I dropped me biscuit. "What?"

"You went to see him yesterday – didn't you?"

"Oh yeah." I picked me biscuit off the floor and I didn't know whether to eat it or not. Normally I would have but some people would think you were disgusting doing that. And then, I didn't want to offend Clara by not eating it in case she thought I thought her house was dirty.

I took a bite and she didn't bat an eyelid.

"So how is he?" She leaned forward in her seat.

This was it. I could tell her he told me to break it off with her. "He's, eh," – she looked so interested – "fine," I finished up.

I couldn't do it.

"Good." Clara took another biscuit and held the packet out to me.

"Naw. Thanks."

"Were your mother and father upset seeing him in prison?"

What was this – twenty questions?

"Nope."

"Not at all?" She sounded surprised.

I shrugged. It was hard talking about things. I normally never did that. "Well, maybe me ma was a bit." I patted me pockets. "D'you mind if I smoke?"

"No."

She watched me light up. Me hands were trembling. I dunno if seeing her was worth it.

Clara reached out and put her hand on me arm. "Why are you so scared all the time?" she asked gently.

"What?" I did a passable scoff.

"It's like, every time I ask you stuff about yourself, you panic or something. In school you're not like that."

I blew out a long stream of smoke. "I'm not scared." I sounded defensive.

"You don't talk much about home or about yourself." She smiled. "The only thing I know about you for sure is that you like cars."

"That's the only thing worth knowing."

She laughed at that and let the subject drop. She didn't know I was telling the truth.

In English class on Monday, Malone said, "I want everyone to listen up."

Everyone kept talking. Tom blew a massive blob of paper right up the class and it landed in the front of her hair. A big roar of laughter followed.

Malone clapped her hands. "It might be in your interests," she said, not sounding very convincing.

"Is it about sex?"

More laughs.

Malone went red. I dunno if it was embarrassment or anger but she marched down the class and caught Kev, the guy who'd said it, by the ear and dumped him outside the door. Slamming the door on him, she didn't see him give her the two fingers.

"Now," she said, walking back up the class again.

"I'm going to go around and ask each one of you who's the person you admire most."

"Riveting," Clara whispered to me.

"Now," Malone settled herself on the top of her desk, "Jane, who's your hero?"

Jane hummed and hawed a bit. "Hitler, Miss," she said.

Everyone cracked up.

Malone pretended not to notice. "And you, Peter?"

"Stalin."

"Tom?"

"Homer Simpson."

"Billy?"

I couldn't think of anything funny, so I said the first answer that came into me head. "Me brother."

It got the biggest laugh of all. I stared around confused. The only one not laughing was Clara. Or Miss Malone. She was staring at me and looking sad.

I felt hurt for Nick.

Malone decided to call a halt to that part of our class. Instead she changed tack. "All of those people mentioned," she began and paused, "most of those people mentioned were powerful people, they got to where they were in the world by . . ." she gazed about expectantly at us. Everyone attempted to look comatose.

"Ambition," Malone said.

"Oh yeah," Tom nodded, trying to sound mega-impressed. "Right, Miss."

"Ambition," someone else said. "Imagine."

Judy, a girl who sat in the front row put up her hand. "Miss? Miss?"

Malone, spotting a chance to calm us all down, turned to Judy. "Yes?"

"I never saw Homer Simpson with a gun, Miss."

A stunned silence.

A big laugh.

"That's *ammunition,* thicko," Tom yelled up at her. "Not ambition!"

Someone clapped. "Good one, Jude!"

"They used guns too," someone else yelled. "Hitler was very fond of guns."

"Stop it!" Malone flapped her arms uselessly about. "Stop now!"

No one took any notice.

"I'm going to talk anyhow," Malone said. "If you don't want to listen you won't know what I'm about to say."

Her logic was stunning.

She picked up a leaflet from her desk. "I got this yesterday in the post. It's an essay competition for young people." She studied us. Another piece of paper embedded itself in her hair courtesy of Tom again. "The title of the essay is 'Ambition'."

"Bor–ring!"

Malone ignored the interruption. She just continued to shout over us all. "The winner will receive a computer for their school and a cash prize of," she scanned the page, "a hundred and fifty pounds."

"That's nothing," someone yelled. "If you wrote for a paper you'd get more than that!"

Malone stared hard at the yeller. "Nevertheless," she said, "I expect an essay on 'Ambition' from you all by next week, all right?"

No one reacted. They all started talking again.

A hundred and fifty quid sounded great to me. I'd write the essay because I had to but there was no way I'd win.

Still . . . a hundred and fifty quid.

I wrote it in study period. It was all right. I just wrote how I'd like to leave school and get a job in a garage. Nothing earth-shattering.

Smoke glared at Whiteser as he entered. "Well?".

Whiteser shrugged. "Donnelly swears he hasn't any names. We got some of the lads in there to give him a going over and still . . ." He let his words hang.

"He's a lying bastard," Smoke said quietly. "Guys like him don't keep knowledge to themselves."

Whiteser shrugged again.

"Put the pressure on. We need a driver we can rely on. We need someone Donnelly knows and can get to." *Smoke viciously stubbed out his fag. "He owes us big-time now."*

Whiteser didn't know what to say. They'd put a hell of a lot of pressure on Nick and he'd sworn he knew no one that could do the job.

"That little feck of a brother he has," Smoke barked, "what's he into?"

Whiteser's mind was blank. Fear made it go blank. He shoved his hand into his jacket and pulled out a ragged bit of paper. "His name's Billy," he read, "He goes to school, works in a garage after school sometimes. Has a girlfriend."

Smoke tapped his chin, considering. "Nick's soft spot," he said gently. Then abruptly, he ordered, "Lose Billy the job. Meet with him." He grinned. "You know the story."

Whiteser nodded

Chapter Nineteen

I went to the garage after school that day. Me bag slung over me shoulder, the sun shining down on me face, it was a nice evening. Paul was underneath the bonnet of a car when I walked in.

"How's it going?" I said.

I tried not to grin as Paul jumped, almost banging his head off the bonnet of the car. "Sore that," I joked, making me way to the back of the garage to change into the spare set of overalls he kept for me.

I threw me schoolbag into the press and began to pull out the overalls.

"Hang on a second, Bill, will you," Paul said. Now it was my turn to jump, the guy was standing right behind me, at me shoulder. I hadn't even heard him follow me down the garage. Turning, I saw that there was a weird look on his face. Sort of sad or ashamed.

"What?" I asked warily.

Paul looked straight at me and then he looked away again. "Was it your brother that stole the bus?"

"What?" I felt me heart beginning to speed up.

"Is your brother the guy that stole the bus a few weeks ago?" Paul asked again. He had his eyebrows quirked and he spoke softly.

Slowly I nodded. "Yeah," I answered, my voice soft too. "So?"

Paul gulped, then he gave a sigh and placed his hand on me shoulder. "Oh, Bill," was all he said.

"What?" Me heart was pounding now. Suddenly I realised how much I loved being in the garage. Maybe I should've told Paul earlier. Maybe now he felt he couldn't trust me. "You *can* trust me," I blurted out, not caring that I sounded pathetic. "Honest."

"It's not that," Paul shook his head and taking his arm from my shoulder turned away.

"So it's all right?" I said, throwing any pride I have out the window. "I can still work here?" I was talking to his back. Like in slow motion, I saw him shake his head.

"I'll work for free," I said, knowing that later I'd hate meself for saying that. "I mean that."

"Billy, don't," Paul sat down and put his head in his hands. I went over towards him and stopped when I saw him raise his head again.

Neither of us said anything, we just looked at each other. I was hoping that if I kept me mouth shut, he'd say everything was fine.

But he didn't.

"I had a visit," he said. "From some guys." He stopped and seemed to want me to say something.

"Yeah?"

"They told me about your brother and they said," Paul looked hard at me, "they said that if I kept you on I'd be making a mistake."

"A mistake?" I didn't know what he was on about. I shook me head. "What?"

Paul stood up. He wiped his hands along the front of his overalls. "It was a threat, I think."

He came nearer to me. "I'm sorry, Bill, it's a risk I can't take."

"I don't understand." I did but I didn't want to. He was dumping me.

"I'm going to have to let you go, Bill," he shrugged. Holding out his hand, he added, "Sorry, mate."

"But . . . but . . ." I clamped me mouth shut. I thought I was going to blubber. Blinking hard and digging me nails into me hand, I managed, "I promise you won't make a mistake."

Paul turned away. "Sorry." He put his two hands on a car bonnet and bowed his head. "I can't take the risk."

I'd liked Paul. I'd trusted him.

The only job I'd ever had was gone.

"Thanks a bunch, Paul."

"Bill . . ."

I didn't even look back as I walked out of the garage. I cursed meself for a fool. Just 'cause he'd been all right I'd trusted him. Well, never again.

When I got home, I tore upstairs. I pulled all me books out of me bag in an effort to locate me English copy. Finding it, I ripped out me Ambition essay and tore it to pieces.

It felt good.

Chapter Twenty

For some weird reason, I knew the guys at the top of the road were waiting for me. They weren't the usual abuse hurlers that stood around and slagged me off on me way to school. These guys looked different, the way they stood didn't look pointless and bored. They looked as if they were waiting. And they were.

As I passed them, they fell into step beside me.

"Hello, Billy."

"Billy."

"Off to school – yeah?"

I said nothing. Maybe if I ignored them, they'd pick on someone else.

They stood one on either side of me and the other one went and started walking in front of the three of us. He was taller than I was, so I couldn't see where I was going.

"Heard you lost your job in the garage yesterday," the guy on me right said. He said it as if he was sad. "That's rough."

Stunned, I stopped walking. I shouldn't have, all three crowded around me.

"You could lose a lot more than a job," the guy with the nose ring said, "Girlfriend, maybe?"

One of the other two scratched his head. "Maybe, indeed."

I felt terror creep up me legs. It crawled up me back and made me shiver. It reached into me hair and made it feel as if it was standing to attention. I gawked at the lads.

Nose-ring took something long and silver from his pocket. A blade flashed upwards. He held it to me chest. "On the other hand, things could be fine – you just tell that brother of yours to come up with some names – yeah?"

I stared, wide-eyed, at them.

"Yeah?" the penknife guy said again.

Slowly I nodded.

Like ice, they melted away from me.

Soon they were blobs in the distance.

I stood there for a long time, sweat dripping from me forehead.

Me mind is blank on what I did that day.

I rang Nick from a pay-phone. I remember that. I told them it was an emergency. When Nick came on line, I just said, "Nick, what's going on?"

He groaned.

"Nick?"

"I'll get you a visitor's pass, Billy," he said. "Come on your own."

Then he hung up.

I was clever enough and copped on enough to arrive home around five, the time I normally got in from school. As I opened the back door into the kitchen, Da stormed out, pulling on his jacket as he did so. He would've knocked me over only I got out of his way on time. "I'm going out," he yelled.

"Blindingly obvious that," Ma shouted.

"Dunno when I'll be back."

"Well, I do!" Ma marched over to him and stopped about a foot from him. "When you're tired, hungry, broke and your clothes rot on your back!" Her voice was really loud, just in case they couldn't hear in Galway, I guess.

"Oh yeah?" Da squared up to her.

"Yeah." Ma said, in her normal voice. Then, spying me, she snapped, "Are you coming in or out?"

"In."

"Then get in!"

Once I was inside, she gave Da a shove and slammed and locked the door on him.

Now, I know our house isn't exactly Little House on the Prairie but Ma and Da very rarely fight. Me ma's not one for confrontation, she normally lets Da away with what he wants to do. She gives out about him behind his back but never to his face. She worries all the time about him but never lets on, except to me. So to hear her yelling after him was a big deal.

I stood watching her as she stomped about the kitchen, shouting all sorts of things about Da at the top of her voice.

Through the frosted glass of the kitchen door, I saw Da sloping away.

Once he had disappeared, Ma seemed to relax. She stopped walking. She just stood, looking upwards with her fists clenched.

"Ma?"

"What?" Snapped out, as usual. Then, she shook her head. "What?" Softer. Then, "What?" like a sob.

Then she started to cry.

I didn't know what to do. Panic and flight came to mind. I wished I was one of those new men who know how to handle things like that, but I didn't. I did want to wrap me arms around her, but I couldn't. She'd probably only push me off anyhow.

"What?" She turned her tear-streaked face to me. "Now what?"

"Nothin'," I shrugged. "Are you all right, like?"

"Do I look all right? Do I?"

I stared hopelessly at her.

She slumped suddenly, like a domino going down. "Sorry," she came towards me and reaching out, she rubbed me arm. "Sorry, Bill." I watched as she walked to the table and sat down. "Shove on the kettle, will you?"

I did and made us some tea.

She sat at the table and I stood by the sink, looking out into the back garden. It's not much of a garden really, more like a jungle. Still, that day, any view was better than the one in our kitchen.

"Do you know what your Da said about Nick?" Ma said, out of the blue.

I shook me head. I didn't want to know either. Their rows were their business.

"That he's a loser," Ma's voice shook. "That he'll always be a loser. That he had a chance to prove himself with his new job and he blew it."

I sought for something to say. "Yeah, well, you know Da . . ."

"It was only a prank," Ma said, ignoring me. "I keep telling him that. Nick is just high-spirited, that's what gets him into so much trouble."

I kept my back to her. I just shrugged.

"He's not like you, Bill," Ma said. "He's not clever like you. You're sensible and normal and ordinary."

I heard her getting up and coming toward me. She stopped behind me and I felt once again her hand on me arm. "I don't worry about you, you can take care of yourself. But Nick . . ." She didn't finish her sentence.

It was nice to know me ma didn't worry about me.

"Poor Nick's always been a sensitive child and your da just picks on him the whole time."

I stared down into me tea and muttered, "Nick'll be fine."

"But will he?" she wailed. "Will he?"

I dumped me tea down the sink. "Yeah," I said. I squeezed her arm. "He will."

Her hug surprised me. "Oh Bill," she breathed. "You're such a good kid."

I liked her holding me, but it was suffocating too. Without trying to hurt her feelings, I pushed her away. "I, eh, gotta do some 'ecker' for school, all right, Ma?"

"Sure."

I could feel her stare on me as I left.

Da came back later that night. I stayed up in me room, listening as he hammered on the front door, ordering Ma to let him in.

Fair play to Ma, she told him that he had to apologise for what he'd said about Nick before he could set a foot inside the hallway.

After about an hour of hurling abuse at her through the letterbox, he gave in. "Sorry – right!" he shouted.

She let him in.

Then she cooked him scrambled eggs and he told her she was the best woman in the world.

The hammering of me heart slowed down.

I spent the rest of the night planning what I was going to say to Clara the next day.

Chapter Twenty-one

Nick was right. No ties. That's the way I should've kept it. This is what I thought when I saw Clara at registration. Totally crap, that's how I felt.

"Hi," she grinned. "What happened to you yesterday?"

"Stuff." I didn't want to look at her.

I think the way I said it startled her. Briefly I wondered if I treated her badly would she break it off with me and save me the trouble?

She continued to look at me and I continued to stare at the table. After a while she turned away and started to chat to one of her millions of mates.

Clara has loads of friends as I mentioned before. It made me feel a bit better about what I was going to do, at least they could all hate me together.

Malone came in and took roll call. When she came to my name she paused. "William," she said, "have you a note for your absence yesterday?" She looked at me over the top of the registration form.

I'd forgotten! Shit!

"Well – have you?"

"Nope."

People laughed. People always laughed at me. I dunno why.

"So what's the story, why were you out?"

"Just . . . you know . . ." I was sliding down me seat

"No William, I don't know," Malone snapped. "So enlighten me."

"Is that humanly possible?"

I guess I said it 'cause I was angry. All I could think of was Clara and Nick and all sorts of weird shit. I didn't care about a crummy note.

"Out!" Malone pointed at the door. She shouted so that she could be heard over everyone laughing.

I don't think Clara laughed.

Slowly I got up from the seat. I picked up me jacket and me bag.

"Get outside and I'll talk to you after," she shouted.

I walked as slowly as I could from the room.

Once outside, I just kept walking.

I spent the day hanging around record shops. Browsing through the CD's and listening to the thumping music until it filled me head.

I headed back to the gates of the school for four-thirty. Lighting up a fag (I nicked a packet from a newsagent's as I was desperate) I leaned against the PE Hall waiting for Clara.

She was walking with two girls from our class –

Mary, a huge fat girl, and Jean, a girl I'd been with once or twice. She hated me now.

All three spotted me at the same time. All three kept coming closer. The last thing I needed was the three of them around.

"Hiya," I nodded to them.

Clara didn't even smile. "Where were you?" she asked. She sounded concerned.

"Eh . . . listen, we'll go on," Mary said softly.

"Yeah," Jean nodded, and then very pointedly, she added, "and remember what I said."

Clara waved them away.

"What did she say?" I asked.

"You don't want to know," Clara answered.

"That bad – huh?"

She didn't reply. Instead, she asked, "So, what happened?" Then. "Malone is furious with you."

I dropped me fag onto the ground and stomped it out. "I don't care," I said.

"I do though." She touched me face. "Billy, what's wrong?"

I pulled away from her. I couldn't have her touch me, it wasn't right. Me heart was sore, I know that sounds crappy, but it's true. It's like all the warm stuff she'd put in me was draining away, squeezing out of me heart. "Nothing's wrong," I said, totally unconvincingly. "Nothing except . . ." I stalled. "Except, well . . . I can't see you anymore."

I swore that when I said it, I'd stare her in the face. Just to make it clear to her.

121

"Have you gone blind or something?" She attempted to giggle. When I didn't grin back she gulped, "Why?"

"Just . . . you know . . . well, I don't want to. I like being free, you know."

"Oh."

"You probably do too," I said, trying to make her feel better.

To me horror, she shook her head. Tears filled up her eyes. "No," she said, "No, I just liked you." A tear slipped down her face.

Without thinking, I touched it and then put me finger to me lips. I wanted to remember the taste of it.

We looked at each other. I dunno what she saw in me eyes but suddenly she smiled, "I know you like me, " she said. "You're not being straight with me."

"Yeah, I am." I made to go.

She put her hand on me arm. "I've fancied you for as long as I can remember, Billy. And I know I shouldn't say stuff like that, but somehow, I think you need to hear it. I'm crazy about you."

Oh God.

I had to do it. Cruel to be kind. "Naw," I said, shaking her off. "You're just crazy, full stop."

With that, I walked off.

I dunno what she looked like, but I could guess. And however bad she felt, it was nothing to how I felt.

For the first time in me life, except for the time Ma scalded me with the tea when I was seven, I cried.

Not for too long though.

Chapter Twenty-two

She was bent over the sweeping brush, pushing a sopping wet cloth along the floor. Streaks of grime from the cloth made the floor stripy-looking. I studied her for a second, before putting on a mournful face and shuffling into the kitchen, holding me stomach.

"Ma?"

"Billy!" Ma stared at me wide-eyed. "Are you not in school?"

I shook me head. "I don't feel so good."

She leaned on her brush and held up her hand. "Don't walk on the floor," she said, "I'm only after washing it."

"I'll have to take the day off," I said, trying to sound weak. "Will you write us a note for tomorrow?"

"Yeah." She turned away and resumed her cleaning.

I didn't know whether to feel hurt or relieved at her massive lack of interest. I decided on relief. At least I wouldn't have to face Clara. Yellow-belly, that's me. All the previous night I'd lain awake, just thinking of her and feeling sad. And this morning, I just knew there was no way I could see her. So when Ma, yet again, failed to wake me for school, I decided not to go in.

"I'll just go and lie down," I said. "On the sofa."

She didn't even reply.

"In front of the telly," I continued. I dunno why I was doing this – I'd got what I wanted, hadn't I?

No answer.

"I'll just grab a packet of crisps first."

She began to hum.

Dejected, I went upstairs.

It was just as well I was off actually 'cause the postman arrived with the visitor's pass from Nick. Even though Ma seemed to be driving with the handbrake on, she would've wondered about me getting a letter. So it all worked out great. Me being sick meant that when I got a dekko at the postman coming up our driveway, I managed to leg it downstairs, grab the envelope just as it was shoved it in our letterbox and get back upstairs again by the time Ma bothered to look to see what had come in the door.

"Funny," I heard her say, "I thought I heard the postman."

The pass was for Saturday afternoon.

It was a weird day at home. Mainly because Ma was acting really strange. She spent the whole day, and I mean the whole day, washing the kitchen floor. Every

124

time I came downstairs, she was doing it. She made no dinner or no tea. In the end, I had to make Da and me some grub.

Opening the kitchen door and crossing over to the presses in order to get some bread for sambos was a major ordeal. Ma followed me about, wiping up after every step I took. "You're messing up the floor," she kept muttering crossly. In the end, I couldn't take it. I left with the sambos half-made.

Then Da tried. After calling me a chicken, he puffed his chest out and strode into the fray. Ma carried on the same with him.

"Mayro," he said, "I know ya worship the ground I walk on, but washing it as well, that's a bit much."

Then he'd laughed his head off and Ma had stared, puzzled at him.

I think it put him in a bad mood that she hadn't laughed because he'd gone out and banged the door and she'd just started cleaning the floor all over again.

I ended up eating his food and mine.

On Friday, I bit the bullet and decided to go to school. I couldn't take another day at home. Ma hadn't bothered to wake me but she'd got up early and was downstairs when I got up.

"How's the patient?" she asked as she filled a bucket with water. "Better?"

"Yeah," I said, feeling a bit happier that she'd asked. "Any chance of a sick note?"

"Every chance." She pointed to a cloth. "Hand me that, would you, Bill."

I gave her the cloth and off she went again. Cleaning the floor.

In the end I wrote the note meself and asked her to sign it.

The worst thing of all was that she hadn't even bothered to make porridge. Well, not bad for me like, but a bad sign, if you know what I mean.

Me heart started to hammer when I arrived outside the classroom door that Friday morning. It was the thoughts of seeing Clara. What would I say? What would she say?

I took a deep breath and, grinning like a loon sauntered into the class and over to me desk, like I didn't care. She didn't look up as I came in, though I did glance down at her. She seemed to be talking to someone though, so maybe she hadn't noticed me.

I dumped me bag on me desk, sat down and folded me arms.

"Decided to pay a visit, did you?" Tom gave me a shove. He was grinning.

"Something like that," I grinned back. I turned towards him so that I wouldn't have to look at Clara.

Tom lowered his voice. He did a nod towards Clara. "Off, is it?" he mouthed.

I didn't like him asking me that. It wasn't his business. I shrugged and rolled me eyes. I mean, there was no way he was going to know how cut up I was.

He gave a splutter of a laugh and mouthed, "Hate that". I grinned too. I knew what he meant. Sitting beside her was going to be awful. I used to love it, now it was spoilt.

Then Malone came in, called roll, and took my sick note. I gave her a real smart-arse grin as I handed it to her but she ignored it. "Thanks," was all she said.

Wagon.

Clara talked to me in English. I guess she felt sorry for me or something.

Malone ate me out of it.

She wanted my essay on ambition.

"It was supposed to be in on Wednesday," she said as she stood over me. "So where is it?"

"I wasn't in on Wednesday," I said, eyeballing her. "I was sick."

A few people laughed.

"You had all last week to do it," she said. "And I'm not taking any excuses."

"And I'm not making any."

I was still staring at her and I could see her cheeks going red, then her ears, then her neck. Her eyes almost hopped out of her face. Everyone was quiet, wondering what was going to happen. I liked it. Everyone looking at me.

"You'll stay behind after school," Malone said, "And you'll stay as long as it takes to write something."

"Ooohh!" someone said. I think it was Tom.

"And," Malone went on. "You can learn all of *Ode to a Nightingale* for next class. Word perfect."

No one laughed at that.

I have to say, I was stomached. Have you ever seen the length of that poem? It's massive so it is. And it's crap. At least I think so. All about some poet wanting to top himself and suddenly he hears this bird singing and writes a poem instead. I could've strangled that flipping nightingale so I could. The guy that wrote the poem died young too, so Malone says. It's just as well, or he might have written something even longer and I'd have had to learn it.

I watched as Malone stalked back up the class. I used to think she was all right but she was just like everyone else.

"At least you've the weekend to learn it," Clara whispered. "It's not as bad as it seems."

I turned to her. She wasn't looking at me, just staring at a page in her English book. I didn't know what to say back. So I just answered, "Yeah."

At least she was still talking to me.

That was the good thing.

Detention was a pain. It was just me and about five losers from some other classes. Malone was supervising. She sat at the top of the room chewing a pen and doing *The Times* complex crossword.

I was chewing me biro too. I hadn't a clue what to write. I thought of what me ambition was, to work in a garage, and then I thought of how crap Paul, a guy I'd really liked, had treated me. I know he said he'd been threatened but I'd bet, if I was from one of the private estates, he wouldn't have folded so easily. He wouldn't have believed bad about me. It all depended on who you were.

And where you came from.

It made me mad angry so it did.

Me mind bubbled with the feeling. And I began to write.

I only hoped it made Malone angry too. I wanted to get at her and all of them.

Chapter Twenty-three

"Ma, any chance of a lend?"

She ignored me.

"Ma?"

She was down on her knees, doing the floor in the kitchen again. This time however, she seemed to be just concentrating on a tiny part of the floor. I'm not making this up, I swear. She was staring intently at the floor and rubbing really hard. The cloth she had in her hand was grey and falling to bits.

I moved in a bit closer to her. "Ma?"

Vaguely, she looked up. Not at me, more like through me. "Huh?"

"Any chance of a lend?"

"I can't get it clean, it keeps getting blacker."

That's what she said. I suppose she was talking about the floor. So I said, "Do you want me to try?"

She leaned back on her hunkers and held out the cloth. I took it and tried to see where she'd been scrubbing. There wasn't a mark on the floor.

"See it?" She pointed at a place.

So I began to rub. I felt stupid but I just wanted her to give up the cleaning. When I'd come in from school on Friday, she'd been cleaning. She'd even kept scrubbing when Da had asked her if she wanted to go for a jar. So, in the end, he'd gone out himself.

The only time she brightened up was when Nick had rung. He'd phoned to see if I'd got the pass but pretended it was to see how Ma was. She'd been delighted. "We'll be in to see you next week," she'd simpered.

Nick had told her he mightn't be able to arrange it.

That had set her cleaning like yer wan in the Mr Sheen ad.

To me, it was as if she thought something was wrong with Nick but she was afraid to mention it. So she cleaned instead.

Anyhow, I guessed I scrubbed the floor for about ten minutes. When I thought I'd done enough, I turned to her. "It's fine now, Ma".

"Is it?" She peered at where I'd worked.

I got a shock when she yanked the cloth from me and yelled, "For God's sake!" And started scrubbing again.

Standing up, I tried to make meself feel better by telling meself that I'd done me best. If she wanted to waste her time cleaning non-existent dirt – fine. But I needed cash.

Her purse was where she always left it, in the pocket of her red coat. Which was where she always left it –

thrown over the chair in front of the telly. I felt like a heel taking the money (I only took three quid) but I *had* asked for it and got no answer.

Shoving the coins into me pocket I walked back into the kitchen. "Ma, I'm going out. Dunno when I'll be back."

She didn't even look at me.

It took the bus over an hour to get to the prison. The last time me, Ma and Da had gone, it hadn't taken that long. Sitting on a bus made me feel uneasy and the longer I had to sit on it, the more jittery I got. By the time it reached the stop for the prison, I was sweating like a pig.

I was worse when I was waiting for me brother to be led into the waiting-room. Me feet kept tapping up and down off the floor. The minute I stopped concentrating on not tapping them, they'd be off again. I kept licking me lips too.

Nick was led in, same as before. He looked all bruised. I think he must've fallen down another load of stairs.

"Hiya." He reached over and patted me on the arm. "How's things?"

"What the hell happened your face?" I'd meant to grin and say hello but the state of him meant that I couldn't. He looked really bad close up. I was just glad Ma wasn't there. She'd have gone mental.

Nick put his finger to his lips and looked about.

Lower, I repeated, "What happened?"

"I'm in deep shit, Bill," he whispered. He put his elbows on the bench and leaned in toward me. He started to scratch his hair. I think it was because he'd started to shake and he didn't want me to see it. "I had a job on, yeah?"

I nodded, to show I was listening.

"A big job." He took a breath. "I'd to get a car and drive it. That's all."

"And?"

He widened his eyes. "And I bleedin' got put in here," he whispered viciously. "So how the hell can the job be done now – huh?"

"But . . ." I stopped. I bit me lip. "Is there no one else . . .?"

Nick pointed to himself. "That's what they keep asking *me*," he said. His voice sounded loud and he curbed it. "They think I can give them a name – *Jesus*." With the last part of the sentence, he put his head in his hands. "They operate like a family," he gulped. "No one can be just *let in*. They want someone I've a hold over so they won't squeal." He looked at me and the desperation in his eyes made me feel sick. "I don't *know* anyone."

"Don't you?"

Nick groaned. "I've no friends, no one will do me a favour." He gave a funny grin. "You know me – no ties."

"And what happens if you . . .?" I couldn't say it. Me mind was numb.

Nick shrugged. "They'll get me." It was the calmest

thing he'd said so far and that's why it chilled me. It was as if I shrunk inside. As if I didn't want to be there. Which I didn't.

The two of us looked at each other and I'm sure I looked as sickened as me brother did. It wasn't just Nick, it was the way me ma'd go if anything happened to him. I don't think she'd get over it. Then there was me. I'd never get over it either. And I'm sure me da, despite everything, would be sad. Or something.

"Is there no one?" I searched for a name.

Nick said nothing.

I don't know who thought of it first. All I know is that I opened my mouth and Nick said "NO!"

Everyone looked.

"No," Nick said again, softer but more urgent. "No way, Bill."

"Why not?" I asked. "It's perfect. I won't squeal and I'm an excellent driver." I was hoping my impression of Dustin Hoffman in *Rainman* would make Nick grin at least.

I don't think he copped on. "Bill," he said. He shook his head and began to breath really heavy. "You are the only good thing to come out of our house." I gave a bit of an uneasy laugh but Nick held up his hand. "You go to school, you read real books, you've got a chance, you know what I mean?" He didn't wait for an answer. "Why the hell do you think I dumped you off that bus? For this? For this?" His voice was rising again. He pointed a finger at me. "You can drive, because I taught you.

Because I wanted you to learn 'cause it's important. But no way," he shook his head, "no way am I going to let you do this."

For the first time ever I was in control with Nick. I didn't like it but I had to say it. "I'm touched," I said, half-mocking, "But Nick, if you don't get a driver, I'm in shit too. They threatened me girlfriend, you know that? They lost me me job. They'll get me too, you know."

"They won't," Nick gulped. "I'll come up with something." He saw the prison officer coming over to him. "Look, the screw's coming," he said. "I've got to go." He stood up. "Don't even think about it," he whispered.

As I watched him being led away, I felt like crying. Not because of what I was going to do but because Nick was part of it now.

Part of the system.

I'd thought 'prison officer', he'd said 'screw'.

Chapter Twenty-four

All that night, it filled up me head. The more I thought of it, the more sense it made. They needed someone, I was that someone. They needed me as much as I needed them. That would be the deal.

I felt cold thinking like that but I had to. If they promised to leave Nick alone, I'd do the job.

I wasn't only doing it for Nick. I knew Ma would never forgive me for leaving Nick in the lurch. She'd hate me and I wouldn't have been able to bear that. Plus, I owed Nick. If I did this job, I'd have no need to beat meself up with guilt every time I saw a bus trundling down the street.

This job would solve a lot of problems for me.

The only obstacle was finding these guys to tell them. I knew Nick wouldn't volunteer me services.

Then I remembered Whiteser. Whiteser had been on the scene that morning when they'd put the proposition to Nick.

All I had to do was locate Whiteser.

And . . . *bingo!*

I got up early Sunday morning. Ma was up before me. She was sitting in the kitchen drinking tea.

"I couldn't sleep," she said. She looked wrecked. Her eyes were all sunk in her head and her hair was greasy. Her face looked whiter than I'd ever seen anyone's face look. She hadn't even bothered to dress, just wore a faded baggy tee-shirt and a tatty dressing-gown.

"There's tea in the pot," she said.

I hadn't planned on hanging about the house. I wanted to get going before I could change me mind. Not that I thought I would, but still, better safe than sorry. "Eh, I'm heading out now," I said.

Ma looked up. She reminded me of a dog that had been whipped. So, because I felt bad for her, I got a cup and poured some tea for meself. Then I sat down beside her. I wished I knew what to say, but I didn't. I didn't even know what was wrong with her except for the fact that she was bothered about Nick. So I said, "Nick's gonna be fine, Ma – honest. He'll be out before you know it."

She stopped staring into her cup long enough to glance at me. Her shoulders shook a bit, like as if she was laughing. "And what'll be for him when he comes out?" she said quietly. "A prison record won't get him another job."

I couldn't answer.

She shook her head. "I can't cope anymore, Billy," she whispered. "My head is too noisy and I keep trying to stop it and quieten it down, but I can't." She grasped me hand. It startled me. It was kinda like the scene from that horror movie, *Carrie*, where the hand comes out of the grave at the end. "I can't cope – what with your Da out spending his cash in Lynch's and Nick banged up. I can't cope." Big fat tears began to run down her face. "And then there's you. What on earth is going to happen to you?"

Me?

"I'll be fine." Stupidly, I felt a sort of thrill that I should get mentioned.

"We've all let you down." Her palm caressed me face. "Your da doesn't understand about education. I can't even help you when you're doing your homework. Every time I look at you I feel guilty." She sniffed and gulped, "And Nick," she continued, "Well, you must be so ashamed."

Me head jerked away. "Ashamed?" Me voice rose and shocked her. "No, Ma, I'm not. I'm proud he's me brother." Her eyes widened and I continued, "I am. I'm proud."

"How can you say that?" Whispered.

"Because it's true." I stood up. "And no one has let me down. Not you, not Da, no one."

I don't know if I imagined it but her shoulders seemed to go from being all tensed up to slumping. She looked back up at me. Her eyes shiny with more tears. "Thank you."

What was she on about? I felt guilty for some reason. "So cheer up, huh?" I gave her an awkward pat on the shoulder and left the kitchen before she could say anything else to make me feel uncomfortable.

About half an hour later I stood outside Whiteser's house. Now, I have to clarify this for yez. Whiteser's house mightn't be where he lived, he just used it as his address. I just hoped that whoever was there would know how to reach him. The house was scruffy. Peeling paint, long grass, dirty windows. Some joker had planted some flowers in the front garden along with all the dirt. Pansies, I think they're called – you know, they're all coloured with big bright petals. Anyhow, the pansies were doing their best to grow, but it wasn't gonna be easy – I mean, super-weeds were clinging to every bit of them. It made me laugh. Whoever done it musta had a weird sense of humour.

The door-bell actually worked. It seemed to keep ringing long after I'd pressed it. For some reason, I wasn't bothered. I'd made up me mind and now I just had to go where it took me. Fate. There was no other way out.

I heard footsteps inside the house and then the door opened.

The most gorgeous girl I had ever seen in me entire life poked her head nervously around the door. I mustn't have looked too threatening because then she revealed the rest of herself. "Wha' do ya want?"

She was about twenty, I guess, with brown shiny hair

straight out of a shampoo add. Big green eyes, gorgeous lips. She wore an old tracksuit, but that only made her face look even more beautiful. I couldn't stop staring at her. This girl was fit.

"Well?" She glared at me and put her hand on her hip. "Hurry up, I can't be standin' here all day waitin' for ya ta open yer bleedin' gob."

"Eh, sorry," I said. Nerves kicked in. "Eh . . . I was looking for Whiteser."

Her eyes narrowed. "And who said you'd find him here?" She gave a sniff.

"So he's not there?"

"Who's asking?"

"Someone he might want to see."

Question for question.

She didn't like me answer. She made to close the door.

"You tell him Nick Donnelly asked me to see him."

Nick's name sparked something. "That piece of shit," she snapped. "What's he to do with you?"

"You tell me where Whiteser is," I said.

She shook her head. "You want to meet Whiteser – you say where." Then hastily, "But I can't promise anything."

"Tomorrow morning," I said. I tried to think of someplace public where nothing would happen me. "Outside the cinema entrance at the square."

"And how will he know you?"

"I'll be the one with the car manual in me hand."

She closed the door.

Chapter Twenty-five

Another bunked school day, which was just as well. I'd done no 'ecker', I hadn't learnt that poem Malone had told me to do. Still, trouble in school was better than standing waiting for Whiteser to show. I had in me hand the biggest car manual I could find about the house. I was afraid Whiteser wouldn't bother turning up, or, if he did, he'd do a runner when he saw it was me.

I stood for about an hour, holding the book and walking up and down. There was only so many times I could pretend interest in the shops and fast food-joints about the place. After a while, I just stood quietly, watching people pass. I was prepared to spend the day there if I had to.

Around eleven, some fella stood beside me. At first I didn't notice anything weird about him but gradually he began to inch nearer. Out of the corner of me eye, I studied him. It wasn't Whiteser – it was one of the fellas that I'd met on me way to school a few days ago. The penknife one. The memory made me stomach lurch.

I waited for him to talk first. I'd some crazy idea that it could all be a coincidence.

"Billy," he said after about ten minutes. "We meet again."

"Where's Whiteser?"

The guy smiled. "He sent me."

"Oh."

"So," he put his arm around me shoulders and began to steer me away from the shop. "What's the story?"

Me hands were getting clammy. This guy carried knives, for Christ's sake. Then I thought that maybe Whiteser did too.

"Well?" Penknife said jovially. "You got a name for us?" He smiled. "After all, you did go and see Nick on Saturday."

Me face must've looked shocked 'cause Penknife laughed. "You think we don't know these things?" he jibed.

"I got a name," I said. I knew it would stop him laughing and it did.

"So how come Nick hasn't told us?" Penknife asked. He was smiling all the time, trying to make out to interested passers-by that we were having a friendly conversation.

I ignored the question. "I'll give you the name if you lay off Nick."

Penknife stopped. He turned to me and the smile slid from his face. "Listen, squirt, you are not in a position to do deals with anyone."

I dunno where I got the courage from. Maybe I was

just throwing myself into the gangster character I was playing or something. I shrugged. "Fine." I made to walk away.

For one horrible, gut-turning moment, I thought he was gonna let me walk off. I dunno whether it was relief or terror I felt when he dug his nails hard into me shoulder. "Just give us the name."

I shrugged him off. Turning to face him, I made me eyes look him straight in the face. "Lay off Nick."

"Did he tell you to say this?"

"Nope."

"We can go into prison and make him give us this name – you know?"

"He won't give it to you."

I could see his fists clench. In the end he said, "Look, I can't promise anything. Your brother has made a few people very angry. Just gimme the name and I'll see what I can do."

I was tempted to tell him to shove it. Instead I said, "You see what you can do and then I'll give you the name."

"Jesus!"

"I'll see you later this afternoon back at the square, all right?" I walked off and left him standing there. Maybe it was in me blood, or just inherited from years of living in me estate, but elation crept through me. I'd done it. For the first time in me life, I'd dipped me toe into the shark pond that swam through everywhere I'd ever known. I'd dipped me toe in and I'd survived.

Nick would too.

Chapter Twenty-six

Smoke held the phone to his ear and listened. His fingers drummed the table as he heard what had happened. Then he smiled. Then he chuckled. Then he laughed out loud.

"I don't know why I didn't think of it myself," he said. "I know what the kid's doing."

Pause while he listened.

"He's going to do the driving for us – don't you see? Nick'd never use him but he'd do it for Nick." Smoke laughed again and thumped his forehead with his rolled-up fist. "Why didn't I see it?" Then, "Tell him we'll lay off Nick. Two Donnellys in the hand is better than one Donnelly in the nick."

His wit made him laugh.

Things were sorted.

"I'll do it." The words were out and I couldn't take them back. I dunno what I expected Penknife to do. Maybe I wanted him to look surprised or to protest or something.

But he didn't say anything. It was almost as if he knew – which he couldn't have. I said it again, to make sure that he'd copped on. "Me. I'll do the driving."

"Heard you the first time." Penknife snapped. He held out a key. "Screw up and you'll pay."

I took the key and said nothing.

"That's the key to where the car is. Nick got us a car the same Sunday he got himself a double-decker bus."

Penknife gave a leery smile but I didn't smile back.

"The reg plate has been changed and she's waiting for her moment of glory." He shoved a piece of paper into me hand. "The first address on that page is where you pick her up. Drive her to the second address and pick us up. Then it's off to the bank to make a substantial withdrawal."

He laughed. It was like he was getting high just thinking about it.

I studied the two addresses. I knew where both were so it wasn't as if I had to map-read or anything. "What bank?" I asked. "Will I know how to get there and how will I know where to drive after . . .?" I stopped. "After..." I finished up.

Penknife stared at me. "You think we're stupid," he snarled. "Like we're going to lay out all the details for you?"

"I just thought . . ."

He shoved his face into mine and the smell off his breath made me pull back. "Don' think," he said. He slapped me on the cheek and said cajolingly, "Just drive, that's your job."

He stood up and glowered down on me. "All will be revealed in the fullness of time," he leered. "Trust me."

Then he was gone, swallowed up in the crowd of shoppers.

I shoved the addresses into me pocket and for the first time it dawned on me that I hadn't been told when I was needed, what time I was needed, nothing. Then it occurred to me just what I had landed meself with. Then I decided that it was better not to think of those things. Just get on with life and pretend like everything was normal.

Chapter Twenty-seven

Everything sure was back to normal in school the next day. All the teachers were queueing up to leap down me throat. I'd no sick note, no 'ecker' done, no poems learnt. I was knee-deep in shit. But it was weird. I didn't care. Everything seemed so small-scale to what I was going to do, I just couldn't take it seriously.

Clara was great. She whispered answers to me during maths or wrote answers down on her copy so that I knew what to say. She even smiled at me once or twice.

At lunch-time, I wandered behind the sports hall for a smoke. A few of the lads were there and I managed to scab two fags from them. Their slagging and craic went over me head, I was busy trying to decide whether to turn up for school that afternoon or not. In the end, after about fifteen minutes, I left.

I was just heading out the school gates when I heard someone shouting out me name.

"Billy!"

The voice made me heart soar and dive at the same time.

Turning around I saw Clara running to catch up with me. She had her bag and coat with her.

I couldn't help the grin that came over me face.

She stood in front of me and smiled too. Then she stopped. "Are you bunking off?" she asked.

"Maybe."

"Well, if you are, so am I."

I laughed. Clara was great but she was not a mitcher. I don't think she'd ever bunked a day in her life. I guess she was a bit of a swot really. But a nice one. "Sure," I nodded. "I believe that one."

"Good!" She fell into step beside me. "Where'll we go?"

I was tempted. Really. But I couldn't. "Look, Clara," I said, trying to sound hard. "I broke it off with you – remember?"

"Yeah. So?"

"So, well . . ." I shook me head. "Look, why are you doing this?" I blurted out.

"Why are you?" she asked back.

She was giving me a funny look. As if she knew something that I didn't. As if she cared about me. The thought of that made me silent. I just clutched me schoolbag harder and stared at her.

"Maybe I'm stupid," she began. She gave a laugh, "I know I am. I never thought I'd be running after some fella who made it plain he didn't want me around." She stopped as if she expected me to say something. When I just continued to stare, she went on, more subdued, "But I liked you, Billy. I did. And I can't switch off. And I know you liked me."

"Yeah but . . ."

"And I know something is wrong and I want to help . . ."

"Clara . . ."

"So let's go and you can tell me." She began to hoist her bag up onto her shoulder.

I couldn't let her go anywhere with me. Instead, I plonked meself down onto the grass and patted it for her to sit beside me. She did and then, delving into her jacket pocket, produced a giant bar of chocolate. "Here," she gave me half.

We ate in silence for a bit, she eating it square by square, me shoving huge chunks wholesale into me mouth while I tried desperately to think of what to say to her. In the end, I said, "Clara, the best thing you can do for me is to stay away."

She stopped eating. "Why?"

For some inane reason, the words of the eighties song *Bird of Paradise* flitted through my brain. Nick was mad into eighties music and he had millions of hit tapes from that time. There was this song, where this guy is letting this bird go. He tells it he wishes he could fly as high as the bird, but he can't. He'll never be able to. All he can do is sigh as he watches the bird fly away.

That's what it was like with me and her.

"'Cause I'm no good for you," I said.

Clara laughed. She gave me a dig. "Let me decide that."

I wished I was like her. Not understanding the stuff I was trying to explain. I shook me head. "It'll be too late then," I said softly. I took the risk of taking her hand. "I'm no good, believe me." She opened her mouth to protest. "The best thing I've ever done is let you go, don't ruin it for me."

Finally the penny dropped. She shook her head. "I can't believe that," she said tearfully. "Why did you ask me out in the first place?"

"'Cause I had cash. I felt good. I thought maybe I could be what you need but I can't." It was funny, telling the truth. Even if those guys hadn't threatened me, this would have happened between me and Clara sooner or later. She was unattainable, too much hard work. I gave a bit of a laugh. "At least now you won't end up hating me. And you would have, you know – I do bad things."

Clara stood up, quite abruptly. "You're not like that," she said firmly. "I don't believe it. You are good, Billy. I know there's good in you."

This was becoming like one of these sloppy films on the telly. I hate them.

I stood up too. "So you stay here," I said. "While I get going."

She didn't follow me.

I hadn't expected her to.

It was really over this time.

I went home. Normally I wouldn't have, I'd have wandered around the shops or messed about in the kid's playground in the park, but Ma was disconnected from things. If I'd told her it was Sunday she'd have believed me.

"Half-day," I said, as I threw me bag across the table. "Teachers' meeting."

"Fine," was her only reply. She was still in her night-dress and she seemed to be floating about the kitchen, like a sleepwalker.

"Where's Da?" I began to root around the press for something to eat. There was nothing. The bread had blue and green patches all over it.

"I don't know," Ma said. She studied me as I foraged for food. "I forgot to get the shopping!" The words sounded surprised, as if she had just remembered. "Imagine." Then she laughed.

It was a strange laugh. Almost as if she was laughing to herself. She'd be fine when Nick came out of prison, I thought.

"D'you want me to go?"

"What?"

"D'you want me to go to the shops for you?"

"Yeah." She floated out of the kitchen and upstairs. I heard her banging her bedroom door. Maybe she was cleaning her room now.

She had a fiver in her purse. Enough to get a few bits of stuff. I changed out of me school uniform and headed to the shops. I knew enough to go to one of the bigger ones as the smaller local shops would fleece me.

I got bread, milk and some cheese and was heading home when Penknife fell into step along with me. He was unbelievable. One minute he wasn't there and the next minute he was. "Be at the second address at half eleven Wednesday morning," he said. Nothing else.

Off he went.

I had to sit down on a wall to compose meself.

Ma was still in bed when I got in. I decided to bring her up some tea and a cheese sambo. Holding the tea in one hand and the plate in the other, I made me way upstairs. I was about to knock on her door when I heard it. Big wrenching sobs. She seemed to be punching her pillow as well. And she was saying something. The same thing over and over and over again. I couldn't make out what it was.

I stood outside her door for a few minutes, trying to decide whether to go in to her. Deep down I knew I wouldn't but it made me feel better about meself to think that maybe I *would* go in. In the end, I turned away and tip-toed down the stairs.

I couldn't even eat. I just sat in the silence of the kitchen for ages.

Da didn't come back until dinner and when he saw no dinner on the table he went back out again.

Ma didn't come downstairs at all.

Nick rang at the weekend. Ma answered the phone. It was the first time she'd been downstairs in days. The house looked a mess, from cleaning and tidying she just seemed to have given up. She cooked nothing, didn't get dressed, just stayed in bed all the time. But Nick's call breathed new life into her.

"Hi," she beamed into the phone. "How's my lad?"

He said something funny because she laughed. Then she said, "Great!" Turning to Da and me she said, "He's got a pass for us next weekend!" She reminded me of a kid in Funderland. More conversation and then the phone was passed to Da. He did his best to be nice to Nick, a super-human effort to please Ma. I think he was beginning to worry about her. He'd even started staying in again, the way he had when Nick was first convicted. But it made no difference to Ma. The only thing that seemed to matter to her was Nick. Eventually the phone was passed to me.

"Hi," I said.

"What in the name of Christ do you think you're playing at?" Nick snarled down the phone.

I kept the grin on my face. "Aw, nothing much," I said. Then added hastily, "Ma and Da are still here."

"I'm telling you not to do it," Nick said. "You listen to me, Bill, you've got to pull out."

"Ma's been a bit down," I said.

"I have not!" That was Ma.

"She worries like mad about you, Nick."

"I don't!" Ma gave me a dig in the back and whispered viciously in my ear. "Don't upset him – hasn't he enough on his plate!"

"We all worry," I said softly. I wanted him to know what he was doing to us. What would happen to us if he let himself get beaten up again. "But we'll do our best to see that you're all right."

"That's the lad!" Da thumped me on the back, nearly cracking my spine.

Nick was silent.

"So take good care – huh?" I said. "Bye now."

Me parents yelled "bye" as well and I hung up.

Part Three

Chapter Twenty-eight

Eleven thirty Wednesday morning. The address was this all-right-looking house in a private estate. I tried to look calm as I rang the bell. I shoved one hand into the pocket of me tracksuit, then I took it out again. I ran me hands through me hair, I rubbed me palms together, I tried to control me breathing.

"Billy!" The door was pulled open and Whiteser stood there. "Come in." He did a classic gangster scout about, looking up and down the road before closing the door.

I stood in the dim hallway wondering how the hell I'd managed to get myself into all this.

"Up here." Whiteser began to climb the stairs and I followed him. He opened a door of what I guess should have been a bedroom but was now an office, and led me inside.

Smoke studied the young fella as he came in. The spit of Nick. You'd know they were brothers, the dark hair, the good looks, only Nick was taller and this fella looked

*young. He watched as the lad got his bearings,
sniggered to himself as the lad pretended to act cool. His
darting eyes gave away everything.*

"This is Smoke," Whiteser was saying.

The kid nodded and Smoke nodded back.

*"You know what happens if you, eh, . . ." Smoke let
the words hang before finishing, "don't perform." He
exhaled a long stream of cigar smoke into the kid's face.*

"Yeah."

*Smoke liked the way the kid said it. He liked the way he
shoved his hands into his track-suit pockets and stared
sullenly up at him. He particularly liked the way the kid
didn't cough as the fumes went up his nose. Maybe, just
maybe, the kid might be better than the brother.*

There were four guys. Whiteser was the only one I knew.
There was a fella called Johnny, who looked mental, I
mean seriously off-the-head mental. He was in charge of
the guns. He didn't even acknowledge me, just sorta
nodded and drifted off into his head again. There was a
fella called Peter. He kept farting all the time. It was
disgusting and no one said anything to him. My guess
was that he'd eggs for his breakfast, 'cause that's the
smell that drifted all over the room. He was scary
though. He looked at me. Up and down. "You more
copped on than your brother?" he snapped.

"Now hold it," the last guy, the one with the massive
cigar said. "Just leave it, Fart, right?"

"Just letting him know the score," Fart, aka Peter,

held up his hands in a gesture of surrender. "Just putting him straight."

"Well, put him straight on what he's gotta do," Smoke said.

Smoke seemed to be the one in charge. He wasn't that old – in his thirties, I guess. Long and lean, with bony hands and yellow fingernails. He had weird eyes though. Pale blue, almost as pale as the whites. And when he looked at me, it was like he knew me. He was scarier than the others.

"See here," Whiteser was pointing to a map, "This is where we are, right?"

I nodded.

"You bring the car here Friday morning at eleven, right?"

"This Friday?"

"Yeah." He looked at me. "This Friday."

"Fine."

It was really going to happen. The shock of it hit me like a bucket of freezing water.

He shook a bit when he realised how soon the job was on. The other's didn't see it but Smoke did. It troubled him a bit. He decided to ask for the kid to stay behind after. Nothing was going to ruin his masterplan, least of all a sixteen-year-old brat.

They were going to hit a bank. At the end of a month all the mortgages came in. Despite credit cards and standing orders, most people paid cash. Incredible.

"You just wait outside in the car," Fart said to me, "Keep the engine running and keep her in gear."

I badly wanted to tell him that I knew how to drive a fecking car but I hadn't the nerve.

"When we come out, this is where we're going."

A red line was drawn on the map showing me where we were to be headed. It was down along the coast. "You let us out here," Fart pointed to a place, farted and continued, "Then you drive to here on your own and get rid of the car. There'll be petrol and matches in the boot."

Dazed, I stared at the map. "Fine."

"Study it well," Whiteser said. "'Cause you won't be bringing it with you."

I picked up the map and it blurred in front of me. I didn't need to look at it, I knew the roads they were talking about. Some were sheer wide joy-riding road, others were dirt tracks, full of mud and crap. "What if it's raining?" I asked.

They all looked at me, even Johnny, who hadn't said a word.

"Some of those roads might bog the car down if it's pissing rain."

Fart almost came across the table at me. "Nick said the car'd be fine," he mouthed slowly, giving me full benefit of his stinking breath. "He said it'd be fine."

"Oh." I hoped Nick was right. "Well, if Nick said it, it must be true."

Whiteser laughed. The others stared stony-faced at me.

"See you Friday," Whiteser put his arm on me elbow and hauled me up from the table.

"Oh, one thing," Fart said. "Grow some stubble, wear a suit, anything to make you look older. We don't want a baby-looking kid in the front seat, it'll only draw attention."

I ignored the comment. I hated being told I looked young.

"Hang on there a second," Smoke spoke and the room was silent.

He gestured with his cigar. "Lads, can you leave Billy and me alone for a few minutes?"

Without question they all slunk from the room.

When the door had closed behind them, I turned to face him.

He was sitting forward in his chair. There was a few seconds silence before he spoke. "I chose your brother," he began, "because he was good, very good at what he did."

Another pause.

"You are second-best. A rookie. Don't let us down, don't even think of it. Do I make myself clear?"

I dunno if he meant to hurt me feelings by telling me I was second-best to Nick. But he didn't. I was used to that. "Yeah," I replied.

Smoke relaxed back into his seat. "It's just when Friday was mentioned you jerked." He shook his head, "I don't like people who show surprise so openly."

I could feel meself going red.

"And I'm not too keen on blushers either," Smoke said. This time though, he sounded amused.

I let me eyes meet his. "Can I go now?"

"And there'll be no cut from the robbery for you."

That annoyed me. "I don't want it." I stared at him straight. Asshole.

"Go." He waved towards the door.

Smoke watched Billy go. He was pleased. Sort of. There was a spark about the kid that hadn't been about Nick. A defiance of some sort. It made him uneasy. Still, he reasoned, the kid loved his brother, there was no way he was going to put him at risk. That was the best hold of all – love.

Walking out of the house into sunshine took me breath away. The air in that house had been thin or something. Everything was dark inside it. I hadn't realised how dark until I'd come outside.

I let the heat of the sun pour over me face. I stripped off me track-suit top and tied it around me waist. All sorts of thoughts tried to crowd into me head but I pushed them away. All except one. By Saturday, it would be over. By Saturday, I'd be free. And Nick'd be safe.

That's all I wanted in the whole world.

Chapter Twenty-nine

The night before the robbery I had terrible nightmares. I dreamed I was running away from something. It was trying to catch me and I suddenly found that I couldn't run. Me legs were working, they were flying along, but I was still getting nowhere. I was pushing so hard and everything was moving in slow motion. Just as the guy who was after me pounced, I woke up.

The relief of being in me own bed, with the snores of me Da coming through from the other room made me weak. I looked at me alarm clock and it read five in the morning. I knew it wasn't, that it had to be at least six or so. Walking quietly, I slipped out of bed and went downstairs. I was glad I had had the dream, it was so terrible that the reality of doing the robbery couldn't match it. At least I knew the car would start, at least I knew how to drive. There was no way, on my part, that things would go wrong.

I was sitting at the table having a cup of tea and a smoke when Da came in.

"How's things?" Da went to pour himself some tea.

I was so gob-smacked at seeing him up early that I couldn't reply.

Da took his cup, filled to the brim with tea, and sat down beside me at the table. "You're up early," he said, "What's the story?"

"So are you," I countered.

Da sighed and seemed to slump. "Findin' it hard to sleep these days, what with your ma and everything."

"Ma?"

Da made a despairing face. "Yeah, your ma." He took a sup of tea and shaking his head continued, "I don't know what to do with her. If I stay in, she cleans and if I go out she won't get up. She'll hardly talk anymore." An upward glance at me. "I don't know."

"She always cleaned when you and Nick were out," I said. "She'd pull masses of stuff from the presses and go mental cleaning until yous came back."

"Not like this," Da said impatiently.

"Yeah," I argued back. "Only now she does it more often and harder."

It wasn't what he wanted to hear. He slammed his fist onto the table and stood up. "Are you trying to make out your ma was mental all along? Are you?"

"No – "

"What kind of a way is that to show respect to your mother – huh?"

If Nick had been there he would've argued with him. Then there would have been a fight. I wasn't into that.

"Yeah, sorry Da, forget it." I despised meself for backing down but in the long run it was easier.

Da relaxed. "I'll try and forget it," he said, self-importantly. "I'll do me best." He jabbed his finger in my direction. "Your ma wasn't always mental, right?"

I hated the way he said that. My ma wasn't mental at all. She was just worried and things were getting too much for her. "When Nick comes out she'll be fine," I said. It was as much for Da's sake as me own. "She's just upset about him."

Da nodded. "That's it. That's it." He beamed at me. "That's why you're in school, you're the clever one."

I drained me cup and glanced at the clock on the kitchen wall. It was eight thirty. Time to head.

I was dressed in me school uniform. I'd put some of Nick's clothes in me bag and was going to change into them when I got to the lock-up. It was only a shirt and tie, the stuff Nick wore when he used to pretend to Ma that he'd a job interview. But they sort of fitted me and I figured those, combined with the stubble on me face might make me look a few years older. If Ma had been herself she would've had a fit, seeing me with stubble, but she hadn't even noticed. Well, she hadn't got out of bed that morning so she would've been doing great to notice, I guess.

I was out the door by nine.

The lock-up was about two miles from me gaff so I decided to walk there. It was a nice morning and I needed silence and time to get me head together.

I find it hard to say exactly how I felt. Fear, obviously. I knew I was scared 'cause me stomach kept turning over and over every time I really let meself think of what I was doing. But I also felt exhilarated. That's not a word I normally use but it's the best one I can think of. I was going to be driving a beaut of a car, that alone thrilled me. I was going to be mixing with a mad bunch of lads that were going to rob a bank. That terrified me and gave me a buzz all at the same time. The buzz came from doing something that would make everyone talk about us, it was like an anger or something waiting to burst out. But at the same time, every part of me knew it was wrong, knew it was bad. But bad things are what bad people do.

You just had to make the best of things.

One good thing about the day is that it wasn't raining. In fact, for late May, the weather was really hotting up. Good weather makes people nicer. No one slagged me off as I headed out of the estate that day. If they had, I would've been ready for them. After this, nothing would make me afraid anymore.

Down through a maze of private houses, across the green, past Paul's garage. He was outside, opening the door of a car and ready to climb inside. We saw each other at the same time. His eyes crinkled up in a grin and he raised his hand. "Billy," he said. "How's the form? No school today?"

I gave him the two fingers. The look on his face made me sad for just a split second. He sorta looked hurt. His hand slowly descended back down and he turned away. That made me sad. I thought he'd give me the two fingers back and call me a little shit or something. But he didn't.

Then I remembered how he'd dumped me out of a job. He didn't care about me so why should I care how he felt?

I needed no one.

The lock-up was easy to find. Just a metal garage door among loads of other metal doors. The key slid in and turned easily. Someone had oiled it well.

Inside the garage it was dim. I felt about on the wall for a light but there was none. It took a few seconds for me eyes to adjust to the dark. And then I saw her. An Alfa Romeo 156. A driving baby. I blessed Nick from the bottom of me heart. It was a real Nick car. I guessed she must've been almost new when he lifted her, She even smelt new when I gained the courage to open her door. This driving job was going to be a pleasure.

The only thing that bothered me was that the car was *so* flash. There was no way I wasn't going to be noticed driving her. I pushed that out of me head, there was no point in getting even more nervous than I was already.

Quickly I changed out of me school clothes. I studied meself in the car mirror. I guessed I'd pass for eighteen or so. An eighteen-year-old rich kid with a da that bought him everything. That's what I'd fantasise as I drove along.

They'd made a key to fit the car. Inserting it into the

ignition, the engine began to burble. The sound of Alfa. A deeply satisfying sound. Opening the garage doors, I reversed the car out.

Then, shutting the lock-up, I took a breath, got into the car and began to drive.

I'd make the most of the lousy situation, then blank it.

Chapter Thirty

Smooth and sleek and purring. Shiny car with a super-stud me behind the wheel. Polished to stand out and catch the light, waxed and greased and oiled. Smell of clean, warm newness. Me, high up in the seat, hoping to be noticed and not noticed. Rolling along, enjoying the feel of the sun through the open window, the voice of Gerry Ryan on the radio. Traffic lights. Red. Feeling a hundred feet tall, like I'm with some gorgeous girl that people keep staring at. Looking straight ahead as if I'm used to being admired. Into gear, release break, clutch up and take off as smooth as melted chocolate.

In control. I've complete control. She responds to every tiny flick of my wrist. Weaving in and out of traffic. *All the Time in the World* by Picture House is playing and I slow down. Lazy, soulful music. All I want to do is drive forever.

But I can't.

Eleven o'clock on the nail I pulled up outside the house. I didn't know whether to get out and knock or just wait for the lads to emerge. I wondered what Nick would do. He'd have stayed.

It was the right option. The door opened and Peter, Johnny and Whiteser came out of the house and strolled down the path towards the car. Whiteser looked cool, sorta like a pop-star, all white hair and shades. Johnny was shuffling crab-like beside him and bringing up the rear was Fart. They opened the car doors and climbed inside. Whitser sat beside me and the other two took the back seats.

Peter and Whiteser nodded to me and I nodded back. Johnny just stared ahead. All three were dressed in jeans and tee-shirts. Johnny's one had a massive nose on the front. *Up yours* written underneath.

I started up the car and, at the same time, Whiteser reached across and turned off the radio. "We like silence," he said.

I said nothing.

As I pulled away from the curb, Johnny spoke up. His voice startled me, so high-pitched, almost like a girl. "Turn left here," he said.

"But –"

"Do what he says," Whiteser ordered.

So I did.

Johnny gave me a few more directions and soon we were outside another house. Someone came out and headed straight for the car. Without a word, a black bag was put into the boot. The person slammed the boot closed and walked off.

"Now," Johnny said, tipping me on the back. "We can go."

Whiteser gave a laugh. He rubbed his hands together and chuckled, "Yeah, let's go."

I inched out from the kerb, driving carefully.

Whitser started fiddling about with some buttons on the dash. "Nice car," he commented.

"Too bloody nice," Peter spoke up from the back. "I mean, let's be honest here, just about every driver on the damn road's looking at us."

"It's fast," I said, trying not to sound aggressive just in case I annoyed them. But I didn't want them to start slagging off Nick.

"Bloody better be," Johnny squeaked. "Better be."

His high voice gave me the creeps.

They soon lost interest in the car when Peter gave the longest, noisiest, smelliest fart I'd ever experienced.

Whiteser, without saying anything, mercifully rolled down the window.

"What you doin' that for?" Peter asked.

"It's a nice day, I'm letting in some air – right?"

"And letting out some too," Johnny squeaked.

Whiteser and Johnny chortled.

"I can't bloody help it if I've Irritable Bowel. Yez could be a bit more sensitive."

"I am being sensitive," Whiteser said pleasantly, "to keeping everybody's breakfast down."

171

"Agh, shag off!"

I tried to ignore them, just tried to pretend that they weren't there, that it was just me and the car. It was hard though when belches and farts and huge whafts of garlic kept coming to intrude on me fantasies.

Eventually, as we neared our "target" they grew silent. Whiteser stayed really still, I don't think he moved for about ten miles solid.

"He's focusing," Peter whispered to me. "He says it relaxes him."

I gave a quick smile and wondered what'd relax me. Me hands were cramping up. I tried to loosen them on the wheel. I took one hand off and started to do finger exercises with it. Then I took the other one off.

"Keep both hands on the shaggin' wheel," Whiteser said calmly. "You want to crash the car on us?"

"It's just me hands –"

"Shut up and drive."

About a mile from the bank, Whiteser took a mobile phone from his pocket and dialled a number. "Yep, we're about five minutes away. Talk in another hour or so."

Five minutes later, I pulled up by the side of the bank, where they'd told me.

If the car didn't ignite from excessive methane levels it was about to from the tension.

I knew if I took me hands from the wheel I'd start shaking. I needed a smoke badly.

Whiteser turned to me. "Keep the engine running."

I nodded. I hoped they couldn't notice the sweat on me forehead. Some of it had started dripping into me eyes. The armpits of Nick's shirt were saturated. I rubbed the back of me arm along me brow, dampening the shirt further.

Whiteser flashed me a brief smile. "Good man," he said. Turning to the others in the back he asked if they were ready.

"Yep." Johnny's face was alight. His teeth gleamed. He pulled out a balaclava and waved it in the air. "Ready when you are."

"Fart?"

"Ready." Peter pulled out his balaclava. "I'm ready." He joined his hands and put them to his lips. He began to speak, low and urgent. "Right lads, you know the score. Take the bag out of the boot, conceal the guns, carry the headgear into the bank. You both know where to stand. Johnny take the right side, Whiteser take the left."

Both of them nodded.

"So lads," Peter paused and took a deep breath, "Let's go for it."

They did some kind of hand-holding, hand-shaking thing.

"Go for it."

"Go for it."

"Show me the money!"

Then they got out, slamming the doors really hard.

I watched them take the bag from the boot, load up and walk casually away. They didn't even look back at me.

I was left on me own in the car with the engine running.

Fifteen minutes later, I heard them. Me mind was on high alert so I heard everything. But the sound of their footsteps hammering down the path, *slam, slam, slam,* towards the car, spurred me into action. I stubbed out me cigarette, revved up the car, her wheels spinning as they opened the doors and flung themselves inside.

Burning rubber and high squeals as we took off.

Careering from side to side, manic laughter and slaps on the back as we drove.

"The look on the bitch's face –"

"Brilliant when Johnny fired the shot into the air."

"Had to, man, had to."

"You didn't but it was class –"

"Should've shoved the gun into her bloody mouth!"

"Got a pile of cash!"

I listened and didn't listen. Their part was done. Mine was still to come. I had to drive and get them safe and then I'd be safe.

"Faster, come on," Whiteser gave me a shove. "Put the foot down!"

I gritted me teeth. I was going as fast as I dared. Once out of the town I'd speed up and show them how it was done but I'd kill someone if I drove any quicker now.

"Go! Go! Go!" Johnny yelled from the back seat. "Come on, before the cops start chasing us."

"Amazing amount of cash," Peter said. "Piles of it."

Their attention was off me again.

I broke red lights, skidded around corners, whizzed by every other car on the road. It was the most brilliant feeling.

Eventually, when it was obvious nothing was tailing us, I slowed down. There was no point in drawing attention to ourselves. After all the speeding, it was as if I was now crawling along.

Whiteser flicked on the radio and lay back in the seat. "Better than sex," he said.

"You must be doing it wrong so," Peter said dryly.

They started slagging each other then.

After about ten minutes, the road began to narrow. Then it disappeared into a mucky track with craters of pot-holes. I pretended I was doing the circuit of Ireland rally and put me foot down. The car bounced and jolted along, dried muck whizzing back behind us.

"Atta man!" Peter cheered from the back-seat.

Whiteser held onto the edge of his seat and forced a smile. "Great driving, Billy," he said. With a jolt I realised he was terrified. So I speeded up. Faster and faster along tiny lanes. The three grew quiet, I think they were afraid I'd lost it. And maybe I had, if I'd met someone coming in the opposite direction we'd all have been mincemeat. But I didn't.

When the road widened again, I slowed down. It was like giving up some power I'd had over them.

"Nearly there," Whiteser said. "There should be three cars waiting for us in the carpark." He leaned over the seat and took the bag of money from Peter. "I'll take care of it."

Johnny began to gather the guns from them.

I swerved as I saw them handing them to him as casual as anything.

"Ever seen a gun before," Johnny waved it at the back of me neck.

"Put the thing down, willya," Whiteser snapped. "We're on open road."

"Click," Johnny said, shoving the pistol into me neck.

I felt the hairs rise on me arms. More sweat broke out on me forehead.

Whiteser slapped Johnny's hand down. "Bloody moron," he hissed.

It was total relief to feel the cold of the gun being taken away. Of course, I knew he wouldn't shoot me, but still, he could have if he'd wanted.

The carpark of a forest parkland loomed ahead. I pulled into it and stopped. Whiteser scanned the grounds without getting out. He pointed to three red cars all parked together just across from us. "There they are," he said.

Johnny and Peter got out of the back and walked briskly over to their cars. Whiteser turned to me. "You know what to do?"

I nodded.

"Good man." He gave me a friendly shove and a quick smile. "Thanks."

Then he too was gone.

I waited until they'd driven off before driving myself. Another mile and it'd be over. I was to drive to a secluded spot, somewhere along the coast and dispose of the car. I had no problem finding the spot, a piece of open ground in the middle of nowhere. Trees sheltered it from the road, there wasn't a person in sight. I pulled in and switched off the engine. I closed me eyes and slumped forward, me head resting on the steering wheel. Then I vomited. I hadn't known I was going to do that, 'cause if I had, I never would have got sick in the car.

It went everywhere. All over Nick's shirt, me jeans, everything.

I felt weak and tired and bad.

But it was over.

Not even a fag could stop the shaking.

I stayed in the car for a while, afraid if I got out I'd collapse or something. When I felt a bit better, I opened the door and went around to the boot. There was a big can of petrol there and like a zombie, I began to throw it over the seats and over the front of the car. I like the smell of petrol.

I took the cigarette lighter I found in the boot and flicked it on.

Me hand was shaking like mad. The lighter went out.

"Damn." I tried again and me hand was so sweaty that it couldn't make the fecking thing light.

I shoved me hand into me pocket and pulled out me matches. I struck one and it lit. Just as I was about to throw it into the car, me hand started to shake again.

Go! Go! Go!

Voices from the estate crammed me head.

I shook it to clear it.

Then Clara's voice, telling me I was good.

Jesus. The match went out. I gulped and struck another one.

Hand shaking badly, I went to throw it. Such a beautiful car. And she'd driven us safely away from the robbery. And I liked cars. And Clara thought I was good.

Go! Go! Go!

And I would be good from now on.

The match was burning me fingers. I dropped it on the ground and shoved me fingers in me mouth to stop them from hurting.

I *couldn't* do it. I couldn't burn the car. I wasn't that bad. I wasn't.

I needed to believe that.

Chapter Thirty-one

I got home later that evening. The house was deserted and I snuck upstairs. Flicking on the immersion I waited for the water to heat. The smell of stale puke was overwhelming even though I'd burned Nick's clothes and put me school uniform back on. The smell of sweat was pretty bad too. I wanted to clean meself up before Ma and Da started asking questions.

"Billy, is that you?"

Ma's voice from the bedroom startled me.

"Eh – yeah?"

"Come in here will you?"

"I can't Ma, I'm eh, having a shower."

"Now, Billy, please."

She sounded determined which was strange. She hadn't sounded like that in weeks. Feeling almost buoyant I opened her bedroom door and peered in. "Yeah?"

"Come in the whole way."

She was sitting up in bed, slightly tidier than she had been with a grim look on her face. The look I always got but Nick never did.

Slowly I inched in, hoping she wouldn't smell me. "What?"

"Don't what me!" Her voice made me jump. "Where the hell have you been?"

"School."

"Liar!" She hoisted herself up in bed. "This arrived in the post today." She said 'this' as if it was an accusation. "It's from your tutor." She looked at me expectantly.

I looked back.

"Don't give me that sulky look," she shouted. "Just don't!"

"Ma –"

She began to cry. She put her head in her hands and cried. I didn't know what was happening. Why was she crying? One minute she was mad, the next . . .

"What have I done?" she sobbed. "I'd so much hope for you. I was so proud of you and now . . ."

"Ma . . . don't."

"I know I've been useless these past few weeks but I trusted you to keep going to school and learning and getting away from this, this," she waved her hand about and her voice rose, "shithole."

"Ma "

"And what do you do?" She stared at me, her eyes all red. "You doss off, you act just like *him*." Big heave.

180

"What have you been doing?" She dropped her gaze. "Is it drugs? Is that it? Drugs?" Her voice was low.

"No!" I was desperate to reassure her. I hated emotion.

She looked at me again. "Billy, don't throw things away. I've told you how bad you make me feel every time I look at you. It's like I'm failing you."

"Come –"

"Don't start failing *yourself*, please."

I had to stop her. If I didn't do something soon, she was going to start crying on me again. Hesitantly I crossed the room and awkwardly wrapped me arms around her. I laid me head on hers and closed me eyes. Me voice tumbled out of me. "From Monday, I'll be back in school, I promise Ma." She felt soft and warm. "Honest."

"Promise you're not on drugs."

"Swear."

Her hand clasped itself about me arm. "And you're not into anything mad?"

"Swear on me life. From Monday I'm back to normal."

"Oh Bill," she put her hand to me face. "I know it's been tough on you, I know I've been useless. But I promise, from now on, if you can make the effort, then so will I."

I didn't know what to say. I felt all funny inside.

"I'm so proud of you." She smiled for a second, then she pulled herself out of me grasp and stared down at the bedcovers. Her voice was quiet as she said, "Every time

I see Nick in that . . . that place, all I can think is that somehow it's my fault."

"Don't be mad." Me arms felt useless now. I wanted to go.

She nodded. "It is my fault." Her finger reached out and traced a flower on the quilt as she spoke. Her voice was low, as if she was trying to control it. "He was always a difficult kid. Always. From day one." She gave a sniff and I prayed that she wouldn't start crying again.

"He never seemed to be happy, not ever. I guess I felt it was my job to make him happy." She shrugged. "But I failed."

"No, Ma."

She continued on as if I wasn't there. I think she needed to talk. "And Brian couldn't stand him, I don't know why, so I had to love him enough for two parents. I kept telling myself he was going to be happy, that someday he'd find something to make him happy." Her voice shook. "I'm finding it hard to face, Billy. The fact that Nick is . . . the way he is. It's very hard to accept."

"Nick's *good, Ma*."

"No," she said abruptly, "No, he's not – he's a waster." She seemed to gain strength from admitting it. "A waster," she said again.

"He's my brother."

"And he's my son," she said. The look on her face was intense. "And so are you," she gave me a watery smile. "I owe you so much, Billy. You're such a good kid. Every time I see you heading to school, I feel I've done something right in my life. And then this came . . ." She held up the letter from Miss Malone. "And it hit me how badly I've screwed up this last while."

"Ma –"

"I'm sorry. I really am."

"Don't," I shook me head. "You're great, Ma. Don't apologise."

Then she reached out and held me. And I held her. And I liked it. I was so tempted to say nothing, just to have her love me like this always, but I had to tell her. It might ruin things between us but I had to tell her. I owed it to Nick. "I was on the bus with him," I said flatly. "Me and Nick took the bus together."

I felt her stiffen. Slowly she unwound her arms from me. "What?" Her voice was dead-sounding. Her eyes searched me face. "What?"

"He wouldn't have got caught only for he stopped the bus and made me get off." I felt as if I was drowning. "He did it for *me,* Ma." I stood up and shoved me hands into me jeans. "And I know if he can do that, then he's not a waster." It was over. She'd hate me now. I turned to go.

I made it all the way to the door before she spoke. "Bill?"

Me hand was on the handle, the door was half open. I didn't want to hang around to hear what she was going to say.

"Billy?"

"What?" I half-turned, not wanting her to see me face.

"Thanks," she said simply. "Thanks for telling me."

It was hard to judge what she meant. "No probs." Again I made to go.

"He knew I'd kill him if anything happened to you – that's why he did it."

I knew neither of us believed that. This was no time for crap. "No, Ma. That's not why he did it."

We looked at each other.

A smile spread itself over her face. "No, I guess not." She shook her head and gave a small laugh.

"So he's not all bad, Ma."

"No."

"So that's that." It was a stupid thing to say. But it was true. That was that.

"I would have though," Ma said gently. Her eyes were studying me and I felt uncomfortable.

"Huh?"

"I would have killed him."

Her words made me feel so strange. All me life, I'd thought she just tolerated me, but maybe she did like me? Maybe she did.

And her liking me was good enough to make me happy. "Thanks," I said.

"No probs," she said back.

I knew we'd never talk like this again. But I knew we'd never have to. I was going to make her proud of me. I was.

I mean, if me ma liked me, then I couldn't be too bad, could I?

Chapter Thirty-two

Ma wrote me a note for school saying that I'd come down with a weird bug and had been laid low. "It's on condition that you keep going to school," she warned as she handed it to me.

Again I swore that I would.

Ma was slowly coming back to normal. She still went overboard on the cleaning but porridge was making its morning appearance in me breakfast bowl once again. And charred chops and cheese-balls were back on the menu for dinner.

Still, every silver lining has a cloud, I suppose.

Da was delighted. Once again he could snooze until midday and spend the afternoon in the bookies. Then he could come home, eat his dinner and watch the races on the telly.

Nick was in great form. We all visited him the weekend after the robbery.

His face was almost bruise-free but he looked thinner than he had before.

"Is the food awful in here, love," Ma asked, all sympathy.

"Jaysus!" Da rolled his eyes.

Nick grinned. "Naw, it's OK. I like it anyhow."

Ma's face tightened. "Oh."

Nick turned to me. "So how's Bill?" he asked.

"He tried bunking off school for a while," Ma announced to the whole room. She gave me a dig. "But we've it all sorted out now."

"Your mother tried bunking off reality for a while too," Da announced. "But she's all sorted out as well."

"Thank you," Ma said in a clipped voice.

"You're very welcome," Da nodded back. Then he put his arm around her shoulder and squeezed her. "Bill and I thought you were going mental."

Nick and I spluttered with laughter. Ma shoved Da off and turned from him. Da tweaked her hair. "No sense of humour at all, have you, Mayro?"

"Well, I must've had – I married you, didn't I?"

Da's laughter boomed out and Ma started laughing too. She was the only person he'd let say things like that to him.

While they were gazing at each other and smiling, Nick winked at me. "Thanks," he mouthed.

I shrugged and looked away. I didn't want him to thank me for anything. It was only what brothers do for each other.

Crimeline did a massive take on the robbery. It'd been on the news too, the day it happened, but I'd been too scared to look at the telly that day. But the night *Crimeline* was on, I hadn't known that the robbery would feature.

We always watched *Crimeline* in our gaff. Da loved it. He liked trying to spot people he knew on the telly. Ten minutes before it came on, he'd make himself a massive pile of sambos. Then, balancing them all along his arm, and carrying a pot of tea or a glass of Guinness he'd settle himself down for the hour in front of the telly. Ma and I usually watched it with him.

Da loved Marian Finucane. He thought she was gorgeous. "Great-looking bird for her age," he kept saying every time her face appeared.

Ma always managed to spot a policeman on the switch that she fancied. One that was normally thirty years younger than her and still in nappies.

"That fella's only just discovered hormones," Da would say every time she managed to pretend to drool.

Crimeline caused a lot of arguments in our gaff.

That night started the same as usual. About ten minutes into it, Marian looking straight at the camera and giving Da a thrill a minute said, "And now, we're hoping for some help solving a robbery which took place in Kildare two weeks ago."

Me heart lurched.

Da rubbed his hands together, "I love a good robbery," he chortled.

Ma rolled her eyes.

"At twelve thirty on 23rd May last, three masked and

armed men entered *The Bank of Ireland* in the main street and took approximately two hundred thousand pounds in cash. They threatened staff and customers and a shot was discharged. They made their getaway in a silver-coloured Alfa Romeo 156." Marian turned to a garda who'd suddenly appeared to sit beside her. "Now Inspector," she said, "How can the public help on this one?"

I wanted to go but I had to stay.

Da and Ma were glued to the telly.

The Inspector gave a cough and began to speak. His voice was deep and rumbley, really solemn. "I've some footage here Marian," he said, "And perhaps someone will recognise the perpetrators from the descriptions I have."

The footage was pretty crap. Black and white and shaky. No one would've recognised the lads, especially with the masks over their faces. Even in the doorway, where their faces were bare, you couldn't know who they were.

"The tape is bad," the Inspector said ponderously. "But we do have descriptions of what the men were wearing." And he began to read them out. "The tallest of the three had a bright green jacket . . ."

"You've one of those," Ma said. I felt sick until I realised she was talking to Da. "Maybe it was you."

"Two hundred grand," Da said. "I wish it had been."

The Inspector finished up his description.

"And now to the car," Marian said, almost making me spew up. "Can you tell us anything about that?"

The Inspector nodded. "The getaway car was, as you said, a brand new Alfa Romeo 156." A picture was shown of the car. "An unusual choice for a robbery. A car like this stands out, so we're hoping for witnesses."

"So why choose a car like that?" Marian asked.

"Cause it's a bleedin' speed maa-chine, Marian," Da talked directly to the telly.

"It's fast," the inspector said. He held up the picture again, "The vehicle in question had false number plates fitted. It had been taken a few weeks earlier from St Stephen's green. On the day of the robbery it was parked alongside the bank, up a one-way street."

"And the driver?"

I began to cough. Panic and dread made the sambo stick in me throat.

"Will you shut-up," Da glowered across the room at me.

Ma handed me a cup of tea. "Drink that up, it'll stop the coughing."

"Some reports we have say he was a young lad. Maybe twenty at most. Dark hair."

Twenty! Suddenly things didn't seem too bad.

"Experienced driver by the way he handled the car. The car was later spotted heading towards Dublin but after that we've no record of it."

"Thank you, Inspector." Marian turned to the camera and began to give a run-down on all the details again. She finished with a plea for information.

"Two hundred grand," Da raised his glass. "Fair play to them."

"Don't be so ridiculous," Ma stood up. "Robbery is robbery. Scum, that's all they are."

"Rich scum," Da said glumly.

I didn't hear much of the rest of the programme after that. I was relieved, to be honest. There was no way they'd catch us now. Even *Crimeline* hadn't much of a clue. The video footage was awful, the car couldn't be traced – it was brill.

I went to bed when they started doing the lost and retrieved property part. Da was trying to convince Ma that he could stick in a claim for some silver antique candlesticks that had been recovered. "It'd be no prob," he said. "All I do is say . . ."

"Night, Bill," Ma called out, interrupting his masterplan mid-flow.

"Night."

"Will you ever listen," Da snapped. "We could make a fortune here."

Ma rolled her eyes and turned back to him.

I smiled. I enjoyed their bickering now, I enjoyed the normality of things.

I slept well that night.

Chapter Thirty-three

Smoke switched off the radio. He lit a cigar and decided to wait another hour. Another hour wouldn't matter. Another hour – just to be sure of his facts.

"Isn't that true, Tom?" I pleaded with Tom to back me up.

"What?" Tom looked at both of us.

I thumbed to Clara, "She doesn't believe me about what Jay said in Biology."

Clara laughed. "That's 'cause you keep making up stuff to tell me."

"No, I don't." I grinned down into her face.

"Yes, you do." She smiled back up into mine.

Me heart turned over and I just wanted to kiss her. "Isn't it true?" I turned back to Tom.

"Yep," Tom nodded. "We all ate ourselves laughing."

"He said that an octopus has eight testicles?" She still sounded doubtful.

"He meant tentacles – d'you see."

"Ohhh."

"Are you thick or wha'?"

She belted me.

Clara and I were back to normal. It was nice to know you could break up with someone and still be mates. Maybe some other time, when me life was straightened out and I had a job and cash, I'd chance me arm again. But for now, it was great just to sit beside her and make her laugh.

And I could, you know. I never realised it before. She laughed at most everything I said.

Malone arrived to take our English class. "Hello," she said and the way she said it stopped us talking. She sounded as if she was high on drugs or something. Happy, actually. She sounded happy.

She virtually bounced up the class and then, hands resting on the desk, she gazed around at us. Her eye eventually came to rest on me. "Billy, come here please."

I gawked around at the rest of the class hoping that they knew what was happening. Everyone looked as puzzled as me. I didn't get up. In fact, I slouched down into my desk and said, "I did nothing".

Malone smiled. "Just get up here."

I guessed from her good humour that whatever I'd done, it had been good. Slowly, I got up from the desk and, with everyone watching me, I walked up the room. Just in case I was in trouble and she was trying to pull a fast one, I shoved me hands in me pockets and looked at her from underneath me eyes. That look drove her mad.

Malone smiled around the room. "I've just received a letter this morning saying that Billy here, " she indicated me just in case the lads didn't know who I was, "has won the Essay on Ambition competition."

"Wha'?"

"Billy?"

"Wha'd he write, Miss?"

"How much does he win?"

The noise in the class was unbelievable. I stood at the top feeling stupid and dazed and thrilled all at the one time.

"One hundred and fifty pounds," Malone announced.

"No way!"

"Oy, Bill. you getting in the first round?"

"I think a clap is in order," Malone shouted over them all

"I think a cheque is in order!" Tom yelled and everyone laughed.

"I haven't got that yet." Malone was getting a bit flustered.

"Tryin' to rob it on him, aren't you, Miss?"

"No I – "

"Watch her, Bill. She'll fleece you."

"I would not!" Malone banged the duster on the blackboard for silence. "Silence!"

Everyone kept talking.

I stood at the top of the room and couldn't say

anything. Clara caught me eye and gave me a big stupid grin. "Well done, you," she mouthed up.

It was the best day of me bleedin' life.

Smoke listened to the radio again an hour later. This time, after he switched it off, he picked up the phone. "I want to see you, Whiteser. Now."

The rest of the day was spent in a sort of daze. All I knew was that the money I won would go to buy me a car. Somehow, I'd get the rest.

Then, I'd get Clara.

The world was in the palm of me hand.

"They found the car," Smoke said softly. He watched Whiteser's reaction. "It's been on the news."

Whiteser shook his head. "The kid got rid of it. He knew what he — "

"They found it among the trees, half-buried. Seems some fella out shooting stumbled across it. There was petrol poured over it but it wasn't burned."

Whiteser shook his head. "I can't — "

"Believe it?" Smoke finished for him. "Well, start believing it. Your fingerprints are going to be all over the bloody thing."

Whiteser closed his eyes.

"I want him picked up. I want him picked up and brought here."

"The kid?"

Smoke nodded. "Who else?"

"He's only a kid, Smoke." Whiteser felt he had to say that.

"He screwed up." Smoke observed Whiteser. "I told him what would happen if he screwed up."

"He's a kid, for Christ's sake."

"He's a mistake we made," Smoke spoke calmly. "If he goes against us on procedure he's a risk we can't have."

Whiteser sighed. "Yeah, you're right." He looked at Smoke. "When do you want him?"

"Today, after school."

When Whiteser had left, Smoke finished his cigar. He sat for a few minutes in silence. Then he picked up the phone and dialled Johnny. "I need a hand with a bit of a problem."

Once again he blessed the day they'd found Johnny.

Epilogue

Ambition

Some people are born in Rolls Royces, Porches, BMWs.
They can drive on the motorways, they can drive on the
roads. One gentle press of a pedal and they speed up, one
tiny flick of a steering wheel and they can overtake.
They can go as fast or as slow as they like. Whatever
they do, it's cool. Wherever they want to go, no matter
where it is, they'll get there. All they have to do is switch
on good old ambition, climb aboard and hey presto,
they've arrived.

Others are born in old reliable Fords, Opels and
Mazdas. No probs. Slog a bit harder, drive the guts outa
their machines and maybe there'll be a place at the
ambition feast for these guys too. OK, so their tyres
aren't as wide, their engines aren't as big, but we'll give
them a chance just the same. Once they can go seventy
on the motorway, they're on the fast lane.

Some other poor suckers are stuck in the thirteen-year-old Lada, or ancient Triumphs. Thirty miles an hour at a push. No motorway driving for them. Holes in the doors, shivers in the engines, but they try just the same. They try just as hard. But the motorway's closed and the other roads terrify the guts outa the machines. Drivers in their Fords or Beemers passing out at speed, overtaking on corners. So these suckers stick to the dirt tracks. Mud and crap bog them down, but it's safe, until you get stuck in some massive pothole that you've made yourself with the grinding of your wheels. And the pothole won't let you up. And the more you try, the more mud and shit stick to your clothes. So you know you'll never get the stains out no matter how hard you wash and clean.

And then everyone knows, no matter how hard you try, no matter how high you get or how fast you drive, everyone knows that you've come via the dirt track 'cause the stains always give you away.

And some Ladas and Triumphs never get out. They try, but crap follows them like a bad smell. And they rot in the holes they've dug for themselves. They rot in the holes they've been pushed into.

And no one knows how high they would've gone.

Or how fast they could've been.

Billy Donnelly. Aged 16.